# Amanda

# My secret erotic stories of sex!

## Collection 1

(4 books in 1 book)

*- BDSM Erotic – Erotcia Novels – Eroctic Adult*
*- Errotic Romance Novels - Erotcia Short*
*Storys - Errotic Taboo - Lesbian Fiction -*

# Amanda Terry Cox

# Table of Contents

# Introduction

**To those who do not know me**

Hi, my name is Amanda and I live in L.A. I'm 38 years old. I've always had a passion for writing, but between us, I didn't used to know what to write.

I've been working for about 10 years in the security field of a large shopping mall. One day, while I was at work, a beautiful woman approached me. I couldn't resist her, and we ended up having sex in the bathroom... Shortly after fucking her, I thought, "That's it. I 'm going to combine two of my passions. I'll write erotica!"

Well, on the pages to follow, you'll find a selection of my spicy stories!

Follow me...

# Brunette in the Bathroom

It makes sense to start with the story that inspired me to write.

It was a quiet Monday afternoon and several of us security staff were feeling surplus to requirements. Whilst it was true that you never really know what's going to happen, we were all pretty confident that security threats were minimal that day. Children (and teenagers!) were in school, the weather was grim and, besides having to keep our eye on a couple of suspicious drug-addicted folk, we'd had very little to do.

I was standing in the entrance to 'Boots', inhaling the women's fragrances that dominated the shop, when I spotted her.

Assuming that she was just about to leave the shop, I tried not to stare at her too obviously as I admired her looks. She had long, brown, wavy hair that almost reached her ass. Her breasts were full and perky and the outline of her nipples poked through her tight, red t-shirt. She wore a short, black skirt and fishnet tights. Her lips were the colour of her t-shirt and she had high-heeled shoes to match. As she walked towards me, I became aware that she was smiling. I smiled politely back, aware that my eyes were filled with lust. Having expected her to walk straight past me, I was surprised when she stopped right next to me. Standing in the entrance to the shop beside me, she looked me up and down.

"Hi," she said, smiling as she spoke and allowing her face to rest in a smile.

"Hi," I said back. I was also smiling, but trying to look stern. As sexy as she was, this might be a security trick. I was on duty and had to remain a little professional. I looked around. There was another security member in the shop. He shrugged at me. There was no threat. She wasn't trying to distract me from a friend of hers. Nobody was with her, stealing anything. I relaxed a little.

"I like your uniform," she said.

I looked down at myself. Like the other security staff, I wore dark blue, black shoes, a light blue shirt with security details on the shoulders and chest and a dark blue tie. It was a manly uniform, but I liked it. Despite the poor weather, it was a hot day, so I didn't wear a jacket.

"It does the trick," I said. My breath was shallow and my stomach rushed with arousal. She looked me up and down again and licked her lips, as though she knew.

"I'm Sharon," she told me.

"Amanda," I replied.

"Nice name," we both said at the same time. We laughed, then she leant over and whispered into my ear.

My eyes widened.

"Pardon?" I said. I wasn't sure if I'd heard her correctly. I certainly didn't want to assume she'd said that, if she'd in fact said something different.

She smirked at me, leant over and repeated herself.

"Fuck me right now."

---

Sharon licked her lips again and stared directly into my eyes. I knew I hadn't misheard her. I looked behind me, into the shop. My friend/colleague was still in there, not looking in our direction any more. He didn't need me, I thought. I started to walk towards the nearby disabled toilet. Sharon followed me.

I walked inside with the kind of confidence that prevents people from noticing you're doing anything unusual. I closed the door behind us both and locked it. Sharon was immediately on her knees.

She unbuttoned my trousers and pulled down my zip. She pulled my trousers down and grabbed my ass. I was wearing a black thong. She pulled that down, then licked my throbbing clit.

Sharon looked up at me as she teased me with her tongue, then settled into a steady rhythm as she pleasured me. The pleasure made me moan as I watched her beautiful eyes looking up at me. They were hazel, almost matching her hair. As she knelt on the floor, her hair almost reached it. She kept staring up at me as she licked me a little faster.

Sharon buried her head into my pussy. She licked all around my vulva and close to my asshole. I was in heaven as she fucked me with her face, but I was desperate to fuck her. The next time she took pulled her head away, I urged her, "Come here."

She stood up and I pushed her against the wall. I lifted her by her thighs, which wrapped around mine. My clit rubbed against her but I wanted to feel her wet pussy. I held her up with one hand whilst exploring between her legs with the other. She wore a tiny thong which was very easy to push to the side. I slid my fingers into her wet, warm pussy. She moaned loudly and so did I.

"Yes," she said, "I want you so badly. I need you. Fuck me. Fuck me, please!"

I slid my finger out of her pussy and licked it. I grabbed onto her thighs again and pushed myself between her legs. Our clits rubbed against each other as we ground together.

We both gasped.

"Yesss!" Sharon moaned as I started to thrust, stimulating both of our clits.

"Yes! Fuck me! Fuck me!" She said.

Her hair flowed down the wall and her breasts pushed into me. We kissed passionately as we fucked and felt heightened pleasure as our eyes closed. I reached around and almost poked my finger into her ass. I pushed my finger into her wet, warm pussy, that was now even more soaked than before. I started to feel as though I was going to come.

I fucked Sharon harder and faster, watching to see if she was about to come. I saw her eyes rolling back and her gasps become more frequent and high-pitched.

"Fuck me," she yelled, "Fuck me!"

I fucked her faster, pushing her body into the wall and moving my hips as quickly as I could. I used all of my strength to push my clit against hers, feeling her warm, welcoming pussy embracing my every move.

"Oh, God," I moaned into her hair, "Fucking Hell, you're so hot!"

"You're so fucking sexy," Sharon moaned, "Oh God, yes! I love feeling your clit against mine. Yes!"

I groaned and kept fucking her. I grabbed at her breasts and pulled her hair. Her entire inner-thigh was soaked with her own lubrication and soaked us both.

Suddenly, Sharon squealed and dug her fingers into my back. It was at that moment that I noticed how long her nails were. I yelped as she did this and felt the tingles of pleasure I was enjoying, growing even more.

I moaned loudly as I felt my body tensing. My vagina began to throb against Sharon's pussy and I felt her shaking. She moaned and screamed with pleasure, into my ear. I felt her vagina continuing to pulsate, as she recovered from her climax.

Still pushed against her, I kissed Sharon again. Her tongue stroked mine and her lips pushed into me hungrily. When I pulled my head away, she gave me the same, cheeky smile she'd given me in the doorway to 'Boots'.

"Thank you," she said.

I pulled away from her and she stood up against the wall. She walked forward into the bathroom and looked in the mirror. She straightened out her skirt, then walked towards the door.

I did up my zip, staring at her wordlessly.

"Just what I needed," she said.

She blew me a kiss, then walked out of the door.

## Hotel Babes

Last summer, my parents invited me to go on holiday with them. It seemed strange, since we hadn't holidayed together since I was a young girl, but I was pleased by the offer and took them up on it.

We decided to go on a beach holiday in Florida. There was a hotel with an on-site pool, a nearby beach and plenty of bars. It sounded perfect to me!

When we arrived, my parents were very tired. They're both in their late 60s, so it's to be expected. We ate an early dinner, then they went to their room at around 9pm. I felt like a naughty schoolgirl, with an opportunity to misbehave.

And that's exactly what I did.

First, I went to one of the nearby bars. I devoured two pints of Peroni, then went for a wander on the beach. It was getting dark, but there were still quite a few girls in bikinis, scattered around.

A couple of them spoke to me and I enjoyed several flirtations. It wasn't until I got back to the hotel, though, that I really got lucky.

Dressed in denim shorts with a black vest top and flip flops, I walked into the hotel bar. I had sunglasses on my head from earlier on, but that wasn't unusual. Almost everyone in there had sunglasses about their person.

There were middle-aged couples, groups of lads, groups of girls and the odd solo person like me. I walked to the bar and ordered a Long Island Ice Tea cocktail. As I waited for it, I became aware of two girls to my right hand side, giggling.

I turned to look at them.

"Something amusing, girls?" I said, jokily. They giggled even more. They looked about 21/22 and were wearing very short dresses. One of them had straight, blonde hair and the other had brown hair that was also straight. They had sunglasses on their heads.

"That's a very naughty drink," the blonde one said, looking at my Long Island Ice Tea.

I looked at it, then passed it to her.

"That's because it's for you," I told her.

She gasped and looked at her friend.

"And another one, please," I asked the bar man.

The bar man looked annoyed, but proceeded to make another cocktail.

"And a pint of Peroni," I added.

He nodded and continued with the Long Island Ice Tea.

"So, what are your two names?" I asked the girls.

"I'm Hattie," said the blonde one, "And I'm Sarah," said the brunette.

I smiled.

"I'm Amanda," I said.

Sarah's drink was served, quickly followed by the Peroni. I told the bar man to charge them to my room, then we went to a table.

---

As we sat and drank, conversation flowed with remarkable ease. The girls told me how they'd recently come out of university, and they were enjoying some 'chill' time.

I told them I was a security guard and they seemed quite impressed.

After our second round of drinks together, Hattie told me that her and Sarah were sharing a room. Would I like to see it?

I followed them to the elevator.

---

The girls had a deluxe room that was very big and impressive. They had a double bed each, a dressing table each and a large bathroom and balcony to share. There was a mini bar in the room and a basket full of light snacks.

"Very nice," I said.

The girls beamed at me.

Sarah went to lie down on what I assume was her bed. I looked at Hattie anxiously. She smiled.

I looked at Sarah. She was also smiling at me. She patted the bed next to her.

"Come here," she said.

I walked to the bed and sat on it. She pulled me into her and immediately kissed me. Her soft lips felt erotic on mine and the skin of her face felt smooth. She wrapped her leg around me and I felt my clit throbbing. She moaned, then pulled her face away to look at her friend.

Hattie climbed onto the bed beside us. She lowered her face into mine and kissed me. I kissed her passionately whilst enjoying Sarah's legs rubbing against mine.

I was so wet.

I couldn't believe my luck.

---

Hattie pushed me down onto the bed, then kissed Sarah on top of me. I watched as the two women grabbed at each other's breasts, kissing with passion and moaning. Hattie's hand reached down and stroked my breast through my vest. I moaned and watched as they continued kissing. Sarah pulled off her dress.

She kneeled up on the bed in her red bra and matching panties. Hattie was still rubbing my nipples and I was moaning with excitement. I wanted to rip off Sarah's bra. And the panties. Hattie still wore her pink dress. When she took her hand away from my tit, I stared as she pulled it off. She had pink lingerie underneath. The girls reached around each other's backs and unhooked each other's bras. Both of them had beautiful, perky breasts. Sarah's were slightly larger than Hattie's, but both were youthful and beautiful. I sat up, desperate to take their tits in my mouth.

Sarah pushed me down and laughed. She picked up her dress and twisted it in her hands. She leaned over me and tied my wrists together, in a knot and then another one. I couldn't separate my hands at all.

Hattie laughed and  pulled off my vest. She slapped my tits playfully. She pulled my shorts down and off, then picked up her dress. After twisting it like Sarah had, she tied my ankles together. I looked down at my restrained legs, then back up at the girls. Their tits were pointy and beautiful. I really wanted to kiss them, to be smothered by them. The girls kissed each other again on top of me. My clit throbbed with desire. The girls lowered themselves, either side of my body, until their tongues were stroking my vulva.

To start with, Sarah licked slowly whilst Hattie licked me quickly. The combination of speeds was incredibly exciting and pleasurable. I moaned loudly as I watched their tongues on me.

Pretty quickly, they settled into the same rhythm. It was fast but sensual. They looked up at me and I saw four pretty eyes with beautiful hair beneath me. I looked further down and saw their asses, still in their red and pink panties. I moaned, then Hattie sucked my clitoris.

I gasped and my head fell back at the sudden, extremely pleasurable sensation. She sucked and licked me, bobbing her head as she did so. Sarah crawled around the bed and pulled off her red panties. She lifted one leg over my head, then sat down. Her pussy was immediately in my mouth.

I licked her hard, throbbing clitoris as she wriggled on my face. She moaned loudly and pushed herself into me. Her pussy was soaking wet and my face became covered in her juices. I licked her clit from side to side, then up and down. I started to lick circular motions on her clit and she gasped and gripped onto my short hair. I did that some more, with increased pressure and speed and she continued gasping.

Hattie still sucked and licked me and I was close to coming in her mouth.

I licked Sarah even fasted and moaned loudly into her. I felt her thighs tightening around my face, almost crushing my cheeks. She screamed and her vagina started to pulsate. She got even wetter than before and pushed into me even more heavily.

"Oh my God," Sarah yelled as she came on my face.

Her pulsating vagina was out of control and her screams were long and deep.

Even after she climbed off my face, I could still feel her wetness and taste her sweet, musky pussy.

Hattie looked up at my soaking face and licked me faster and harder. It was almost instantly that I knew I was going to come.

"Oh God," I gasped as I looked down at her. Sarah, now naked, was crawling behind her. She was pulling Hattie's panties down as she licked me. As Hattie's ass was bared and she licked me even harder, I knew that it was happening.

"I'm coming," I managed to blurt out, before I orgasmed powerfully on Hattie's face.

---

As I lay, shaking and recovering, Hattie and Sarah started to kiss again. Their naked bodies looked beautiful together. Sarah's leg wrapped around Hattie's and they started to grind together. Both girls moaned as they tribbed in front of me. Sarah reached across and pushed her finger into my vagina.

Her and Hattie continued to fuck each other as she fingered me. As I watched the display and she fucked me with her finger, I moaned. My clit was sensitive but it still throbbed with excitement. She pushed another finger in as her and her friend rubbed their clits together.

"Lick me," I heard Hattie say to Sarah. Sarah nodded, then looked at me again. She climbed onto me, reverse-cowgirl, then Hattie stood up on the bed.

Whilst Sarah rode me, she licked Hattie's clit. Hattie was balancing by holding onto Sarah's shoulders, so both of their weights were on me. The force with which Sarah fucked me doubled as she licked Hattie and I moaned loudly as both women moaned beneath me. Sarah's ass bounced on my pelvis and her brown hair jumped around her back. I longed to touch the women, but with my restrained wrists, all I could do was poke Sarah with my closed fists.

I felt myself close to coming again.

Sarah's moans got louder into Hattie's clit and Hattie, still balancing with the help of Sarah's shoulders, looked as though she was about to collapse.

"Oh my God!" Hattie screamed as she lowered herself onto Hattie, all of her weight landing on us and her legs around Sarah's thighs. Sarah continued to fuck me. I screamed and gasped. I felt myself coming even harder than before and was breathless as exploded beneath Sarah. I saw blackness before my eyes and thought I was going to pass out.

The women climbed off me and kissed each other again. They looked at me playfully, then whispered to each other. Sarah pulled her dress back on.

"We'll see you later," she said.

I shook my head, then Hattie put her dress on, too. Neither of the girls bothered with their underwear.

"Back soon," she said.

I was left alone, tied up in Hattie and Sarah's hotel room.

# Late Night Wanderer

Sometimes, I like to go out walking on my own. I find that it helps me to think, to be creative and to prepare myself for a good night's sleep.

I used to think that it was during one of my late night wanders that I'd find my inspiration for what to write about. Whilst that wasn't strictly true, one night it was...

---

It was about 11pm and I was a couple of streets away from my apartment. I hadn't seen a single person out and about on the quiet roads, and I thought it was going to stay that way. I was proven wrong, when I reached my apartment building.

"I've forgotten my keys!" The woman said. She looked a little younger than me, and she looked familiar. I knew straight away that she lived in the same block of apartments as I did.

"Amanda to the rescue," I said to her, jokily. She smiled gratefully and I let us both in. It was in the harsh light of the hallway that I saw she still looked anxious.

"Do you not have your apartment key?" I asked her, knowing the answer.

She shook her head.

"Don't worry," I told her, "I have a sofa bed. You can stay, it's no problem. Have you eaten? Would you like anything to drink?"

The woman shook her head some more.

"I couldn't," she said, "Thank you, but I couldn't. That would be so rude of me. It's my own fault; I've been so silly!"

I put my arm on her shoulder, reassuringly.

"Don't be silly," I told her. "We've all done it! You got lucky, because you don't need to sleep in the hall all night. Come on, it's no problem at all."

Hesitantly, she followed me into my apartment. As soon as we got inside, she seemed to relax a little.

"It's just like mine," she said, smiling.

"I'm Stephanie," she told me, holding out her hand to shake mine.

I shook her hand. "Amanda," I told her. "Can I take your jacket?"

Stephanie took of her leather jacket and handed it to me.

"Thank you so much for this," she said, "I'll be gone first thing in the morning. I'll even let myself out, before you're up."

I shook my head. "I'm getting up at 6," I told her, "Honestly, it's fine. You'll be able to get hold of the landlord at around 8, I would expect."

She nodded.

"That's what happened last time," she said.

I laughed.

"You've done this before?"

She nodded timidly, then laughed with me.

---

We sat in my living room together for more than an hour, drinking a bottle of red I had in the kitchen. She told me how she'd been out for a late night walk to try and find creativity. She was a songwriter. I asked her if she'd been successful and she'd laughed and shrugged her shoulders. Stephanie was mysterious.

She wore a knee-length, flowery, hippie-style dress, with brown boots. She'd taken the brown boots off immediately after stepping into my apartment and she had no socks underneath. Her nails were painted blue and she wore an anklet.

"Thank you so much for tonight," she said to me, when it got close to 12.30. I looked at the time and raised my eyebrows.

"Yikes," I said, "I really should be going to bed."

She looked into my eyes.

"Would you like to take my bed," I asked, "Or the sofa bed?"

"Which one would you like?" She said, still staring at me.

"I really don't mind," I said.

"Go on, you choose,"

I shrugged my shoulders, like she had when I'd asked her about the inspiration. She seemed to notice the mimicking and smiled softly.

She kept staring at me, so I eventually answered, "I'll take my bed."

She smiled more. "Then I'd like to sleep in your bed, too."

"Oh," I said, pretending not to know what she meant. Well, I couldn't be sure, after all.

"I'll take the sofa bed, then," I said.

She laughed.

"Then I'll take the sofa bed," she said.

Our faces got closer together and the next thing we knew, we were kissing.

---

Stephanie's tongue entered my mouth and twisted around my tongue. Her lips pressed into mine and her hands ran down my front. She seemed amazingly horny as she pushed her body into me and I pulled her in even closer. Stephanie wrapped her bare leg around me and straddled me on the sofa.

"Come on," I said, "Let's go to my bedroom."

I carried Stephanie into my room and lowered her onto the bed. I pushed her softly backwards and kissed her inner thigh. I licked her and pulled the dress of her skirt up completely. Her legs were smooth and shaven and I quickly found out that her pussy was, too. I pulled down her purple panties and threw them on the floor of my bedroom. My tongue flicked at the entry to her vagina and I teased her.

Stephanie kicked her legs as I teased her with my tongue and tried to pull my head into her. I reached up her dress and grabbed onto her breasts. She didn't wear a bra. I squeezed her nipples between my fingers and started to lick her clit. She moaned loudly and I felt her body relax.

I licked her softly and steadily, moaning myself into her pussy as I enjoyed its warmth and wetness. Stephanie's legs wrapped around me as she succumbed to the pleasure she received. Her moans were regular but grew with intensity, the harder I pushed my tongue into her. When I teased around her hole again, she gasped and her legs tensed. Then, when I licked her clit, I felt her legs relax again.

I had fun licking Stephanie, but I wanted to fuck her. My clit and my pussy was soaked. I kneeled up on the bed and Stephanie's hands immediately grabbed at my jeans.

She unbuttoned and unzipped them in a flash, then pulled my jeans and knickers down in one got. She pulled my blouse over my head, then pulled my naked body down on top of her. She unhooked my bra and threw it to the side of the bed. Our tits pushed together. I pulled her dress over her head and kissed her. Her brown, curly hair covered my pillow. I kissed her breasts, one by one, then squeezed her nipples again. As she moaned, I lowered my clit towards hers. She looked up at me longingly and I started to grind against her. We both moaned loudly and our breathing got heavier.

"Oh God, yes," Stephanie moaned as I thrust deeply in and out of her. Her fingers gripped into my back and she thrust her hips with mine.

As we established a shared rhythm, I could tell she was a musician. Even her moans sounded song-like.

"Amanda," she sang as we fucked. Her voice was so beautiful, I felt like that alone could provide me with all the sensual pleasure I could crave.

As I ground against her clit, she seemed angelic. Stephanie thrust with me and we reached a climax, steadily, together. Her hands explored my chest, back, buttocks and vagina. Her clit banged against mine repetitively and she screamed each time.

When she looked into my eye and mouthed, "I'm coming," I already knew that I was doing the same.

I felt my face distorting as I watched her mouth twist. She gasped loudly and her body began to buck. She shook violently beneath me as she came, moaning and gripping my back.

I came with her and kissed her deeply again. When our lips parted, she looked straight into my eyes.

I climbed off her and kissed her neck.

The next thing either of us knew, it was 6am.

# Stranger on the Train

It was the beginning of an hour-long train journey. I'd just taken my seat on the almost-empty train, when I became aware of a woman's face, staring at me in the window.

I looked at her, through the window and winked. I wasn't certain, as usual, that she was actually looking. When she winked back, I became pretty sure.

About 1 minute later, the woman – who sat in front of me – pushed a piece of paper through the back of the seat. I accepted it from her and opened it up.

"Toilets. Five minutes. X"

I looked at her again in the window. She winked again. I looked at my watch and decided to go to the toilets, four minutes from then.

---

When four minutes had passed, I stood up. I walked as casually as I could to the toilet at the end of the carriage. It was vacant. I opened the door and turned around. She was walking just behind me.

I walked into the cubicle and left it ajar. Several seconds later, it was being pushed again. I let the woman in. We locked the door.

---

The stranger on the train had red hair and tattoos. She wore all black and had a nose piercing. I also wore black, but not in the same way. I simply had blue jeans and a black t-shirt on. With Converse trainers. She pushed me immediately down onto the toilet. I was relieved that the lid was down.

"I can tell you're a lesbian. Take off your jeans," she instructed me, stepping out of her panties. Here was a woman who knew what she wanted, I thought. I unzipped my jeans, as instructed, then watched as she climbed on top of me.

The woman fucked me frantically from the get-go. Her pussy was tight and soaking wet. She lowered herself onto mine and pushed herself into me. She moaned quite loudly, and I was worried that people would hear.

"Yes!" She moaned, "Oh God yes! I love your hard little clit. Yes that feels so good against mine. Oh! Oh! God!"

I groaned as she fucked me. Her tight, youthful body was using mine like a sex toy. It felt surreal, I wasn't sure if I was dreaming.

Suddenly, the girl slapped me around the face. I knew then that I couldn't be dreaming. She did it again and again, then moaned even louder as she fucked me harder.

I thrust into her slightly but she was completely in control. She even wrapped her hands around my throat at one point, shortly before she was about to come.

She bounced on me and strangled me. I was short of breath, struggling to breathe at all. My vision became blurred and my ability to think vanished. All I could do was feel. I her pussy's wetness soaking my crotch as she fucked me fast. I heard her moans and gasps. I felt more pleasure. More pleasure. I was coming. I felt it. I was coming.

She let go of my throat as I leant back and gasped. She moaned with contentment and her face relaxed into a smile. She climbed off me.

Before I had time to pull up my jeans, the woman had unlocked the bathroom door. I locked it hurriedly after she walked out, then exhaled loudly.

I spent several minutes, worried to come out of the cubicle before I eventually did. When I returned to my seat, the woman was nowhere to be seen.

## Extras...

I'm not the kind of girl who pays for sexual services. Ever. I just wanted to make sure that you know that, before I go on to tell you my next story.

I was at work one day, when a beautiful woman approached me. She was about 28 and had long, pristine blonde hair. Her nails were long and manicured, her make-up looked as though it had done professionally and her clothes – which looked as though they were part of a uniform – fitted her perfectly.

"Hey," she said as she walked up to me, with flyers in her hand.

"Hello," I'd said. She shoved a flyer into my hand.

"We have a new place in the mall," she said, "Offering massage services. You look as though you might be interested."

I laughed out loud.

"I look as though I might be interested?" I repeated. She was cheeky, I thought. And incorrect! I'd never had a massage in my life.

"Yes, miss," she said.

"I've never had a massage in my life," I told her.

"That's why you need one," she quickly replied.

She was witty. I liked her. I wanted a massage. With her.

"Hmm," I said, looking at the flyer.

"These are our introductory offers," she said, "You won't find prices like it anywhere else. And the services are... exquisite."

As she said the word "exquisite," her tongue rolled over her teeth. I was lusting heavily over her and couldn't help but agree.

"Okay," I said.

As soon as I said that, she pulled out her phone.

"Excellent," she said, "What would you like us to book you in for? A full body massage?"

The thought of this woman giving me a full body massage made me tingle all over.

"Yes please," I said croakily.

She continued to click in her phone.

"What time do you finish?" She asked, "Or, do you have a break at all?"

I opened my mouth. For whatever reason, I hadn't expected her to book me in on the same day.

"Um, I finish at 6pm today," I told her.

She beamed.

"Excellent," she said, "How about if we book you in for 6.15?"

I shrugged my shoulders. I was aware that I was grinning and I felt extremely elated.

"Okay!" I said, "See you then!" She said nothing, but waved at me, wiggling her fingers. She walked away and I stared at her ass.

"Full body massage" echoed in my head.

---

When 6 o' clock came, I looked again at the flyer that I'd shoved into my pocket.

'Bubbles' was the name of the massage parlour. It sounded friendly, I thought.

My mind drifted back to the blonde, beautiful woman who had approached me. Even her smell lingered in her memory. She had smelt both fresh and slightly spicy. I imagined her hands on my body and felt my clit twitching. I walked to 'Bubbles'.

When I got there, a dark-haired girl of about 21 greeted me on reception.

"Claire told us about you," she said, giggling. "You're going to be with Leanne."

As she said that, my heart stopped. Claire was the one who had told her about me, but I was going to be with Leanne?

"Excuse me?" I asked. I was all too aware that a bead of sweat fell down my face.

"Please take a seat," smiled the young receptionist.

I sat down, less excited than I'd felt before. I looked again at the flyer from my pocket. The introductory cost of the full body massage was $50. That seemed a lot, to me, for something I didn't actually want. Not if it wasn't with Claire!

I considered standing up and leaving, when I saw Leanne.

"Amanda?" The silky voice said. She was a red-headed beauty, who looked about 25. Her nails were red and long and I wondered how she could massage with nails of that length. She wore the same uniform as Claire had: a pink, small blouse with a black skirt with a slit. She wore black, high-heeled sandals with toe-nails that were the same red as her fingernails.

"Hello," I said. I needed a drink of water.

"I'm Leanne," she said, leading me in to her private massage room. She walked to the side of a long, narrow bed which was what I assumed I would be lying on.

"So, Claire tells me this will be your first massage?" She asked, smiling sympathetically.

I nodded. Wasn't it normal? I wondered. Hadn't most people not had a massage before?

She nodded back at me, holding her sympathetic expression.

"You look like you really need to wind down and completely relax," she said, "I can help you to do that."

I nodded. I imagined her licking my clit. I felt it hard in my panties.

"Would you like to be naked, or to wear your briefs?" She asked.

I didn't know.

"I don't know," I said, "What's normal?"

She smiled softly. There still seemed to be a tinge of sympathy in her expression.

"Well," she said, "It's important that you do what you feel comfortable with."

She looked at my breats, then up into my eyes again.

"I think naked," she said.

I took of my clothes, whilst she mixed oils.

---

When Emily turned around, I was already lying, face down on the bed. She put a thin, papery towel over my buttocks, then picked up a bowl of oils she'd just mixed.

"I'm going to start on your back," she said smoothly, "Is that okay?"

"That's great," I murmured into the bed. Before approaching me, she'd put on some soothing, atmospheric music. I already felt relaxed.

I was aware of her placing the bowl next to me and rubbing her hands together.

"Okay," she said softly as her hands ran down my back for the first time. Covered in oils, her hands stroked me smoothly. She pushed into my back and I heard myself involuntarily groaning. She rubbed more oil into her hands, then focused on my shoulders.

"You have been very tense," she said, "It must be a stressful job, working in security."

I laughed. It was very rarely stressful.

"Yes, that's it," she said, "Relax. Relax. I'll take you to a happy place."

Emily spent a lot of time massaging my shoulders, then returned to my back. Slowly and gently, she eased the thin towel away from my buttocks, and rubbed me there.

"Is that okay?" she asked softly.

I grunted and nodded my head.

She pushed her hands into my buttocks, providing pleasurable sensations I'd never felt before. Her thumbs were close to the edge of my anus and the pressure she was putting on made me moan with pleasure. I felt my clit throbbing as she massaged my ass, I became more and more aroused.

"Is that good?" she asked again. I nodded and grunted some more.

Emily removed the towel completely and ran her hands down my thighs. She squeezed more oil onto her hands and rubbed them together for a long time. When her touch returned to me, I couldn't help but moan again.

She ran her soft, oil-covered hands down the back of my legs, then back up again. She pushed with her fingers and with the balls of her hands. Her palms pressed into my thighs, then her hands returned to my ass. She stroked up my back again, then around my shoulders and neck. She leant over to me and whispered into my ear.

"Would you like to turn around?"

I turned around without questioning it. I'd have done anything Emily had asked me to: utterly seduced.

When I turned my body on the bed, so I lay on my oily back, she stood over me. She looked down at my glistening pussy, wet with arousal.

"Sorr-" I started to say.

"Shh," she said, putting her finger over my lips. "I do extras. It's okay."

I nodded and watched as she lowered her face down to my throbbing clitoris. She kissed it teasingly, then stuck her tongue out and licked it. As though she were giving my clit its own massage, she spent a long time lightly going over and around it with her tongue. I moaned and groaned with both pleasure and frustration. She was teasing me and she was enjoying it. I was enjoying it, too. Her red hair shone in the light of the room and her green eyes enchanted me.

She kept her tongue out and her eyes on mine as she ran her mouth down the entire length of my pussy. When she found my hole, she stuck her tongue inside.

"Oh, God," I moaned as she penetrated me with her tongue. Her strong, masseuse's hand reached for my clit and started to rub it.

"Oh my God," I gasped. She rubbed my clit with the perfect amount of pressure as she fucked me with her tongue. She licked around the edge of my hole and down to my anus, like her thumb had done before. I moaned loudly as her tongue flickered there. It was a tingling, euphoric sensation that I've never experienced before or since.

She licked up and down my asshole, then pushed her tongue into my pussy again.

"Would you like a happy ending?" She asked me.

"Yes please," I nodded shamelessly. I knew that by 'happy ending', she meant that she was going to charge me, but it was too late – way too late – to decline.

She licked my clit hard.

---

Emily's head moved from side to side beneath me as she licked my clit. I watched her glowing red hair as I felt the extreme sensual pleasure she gave so naturally. Her tongue sporadically flicked me as she licked, making me gasp with surprise and delight every time.

She gradually got faster and faster and seemed to share my journey to climax. This wasn't just a woman giving a service.

She looked into my eyes and squeezed my thighs as she licked me. When my moans got louder, her licks got even harder. She dug her nails into my skin and my head fell back as the pleasure took over me. She dug them in harder, then slapped my ass. I moaned loudly and she spanked me again. Her finger poked the edge of my anus, further than before. She licked me harder and faster. She licked even faster. Faster. I came into her mouth and was left gasping, breathless on the bed.

Emily licked her lips and smiled at me as she pulled her head away.

"I like you," she said.

## They looked like Twins

I was relaxing in my apartment, listening to some '80s music I remembered from when I was very small, when there was a knock on the door.

"Stephanie, hi!"

Stephanie smiled at me. She looked amazing, as always. She wore a purple, short dress with black leggings and flip flops.

"You look good," I told her.

She leant forward and kissed me.

"You too," she said, smiling cheekily.

"May I come in?"

"Of course!" I told her.

Stephanie and I had established quite a close friendship, since the night she locked herself out. The sex had turned out to not be a one-off, and I wondered, hopefully, if that might be why she was visiting.

"What's up?" I asked her, walking through to the kitchen. She followed me in there.

"Would you like a drink?" I asked her, "Tea, coffee, wine?"

It was only 1.30, but it was Saturday.

"Coffee would be great," she said. She looked around my kitchen approvingly. "It's clean in here," she said.

I felt a little proud. I'd actually just cleaned it.

"Thanks," I said, pulling out the cups.

"Aaron," Stephanie said, making ringlets in her brown hair with her finger.

"Yes?" I asked. I looked at her tenderly. She was beautiful, gentle and seemed fragile. I wondered what songs she'd been writing, recently.

"I have a friend coming over tonight," she said, "She'd like to meet you."

I was surprised.

"Oh," I said, "Sure. That sounds cool."

Stephanie nodded and looked at me. I wasn't sure what she was trying to tell me.

"Do you fancy going for drinks with us, around 8?" She asked.

I nodded. I really did feel like going for drinks.

"I'd love to!" I said.

Stephanie seemed pleased. We drank the coffee together and she commented on the music. I found out that she preferred Bronski Beat to Depeche Mode, which surprised me but I found it cool.

She went back to her apartment after coffee, with the promise that she'd see me at 8pm.

---

I didn't do much for the rest of the day, but I did wonder, lots of times, why Stephanie's friend wanted to meet me? We weren't an *item*, or were we? The way Stephanie had looked at me, naughtily, suggested there was something I should be picking up on. I hadn't picked up on it. What was going on? What did the night have in store?

---

When Stephanie knocked on my door, just before 8, I answered immediately. I'd dressed in a black, low cut top and black skinny jeans. I wore black shoes and had straightened by side-fringe and styled and sprayed my spiky hair.

"Hey!" She said, "This is Ellie!"

I looked next to Stephanie, at Ellie, then blinked.

"Oh my! Gosh, wow!" I said, "Stephanie! You didn't tell me you had a twin!"

Both girls laughed loudly.

"We always get that!" Said Stephanie, holding her sides from laughter.

The two women were dressed similarly, though not the same, in silky, short dresses. I'd never seen Stephanie dressed like that before. They had high-heeled sandals on and both of them wore their hair down. Stephanie's hair seemed somehow fuller than usual. Ellie's looked the same.

"I can't believe it!" I said, "So are you sisters?"

They both shook their heads.

"Come on!" I said, "You are! You have to be! Are you sure you weren't separated at birth?"

"We have entirely different birthdays," Ellie said.

I shrugged and shook my head. I couldn't believe that they weren't twins.

"Come on," Stephanie said, "I'm desperate for a G&T.

---

When we got to the lively, student-friendly bar, Stephanie insisted on buying the first round of drinks. She ordered herself a double gin and tonic, Ellie had a white wine and I had a pint of Fosters. We sat in a small booth.

"I feel a bit old for this place," Ellie said.

"Me too," I agreed.

Stephanie pretend-slapped us both.

"Stop being fogies!" She said.

I laughed and sipped my pint.

I was sat on my own bench, whilst those two sat together in front of me. I still wasn't over how alike they looked.

After several minutes of chatting and drinking quickly, I felt a foot on my leg. Assuming it was Stephanie's, I smiled at her. She looked at Ellie and laughed. I realised that I was almost directly opposite Ellie.

I looked at Ellie and she smiled at me. The foot on my leg moved further up towards my groin. I raised my eyebrows and looked at Stephanie. She smiled at me. She knew.

"Ellie has been dying to meet you, after some of the things I've told her about you," Stephanie said.

I looked at Ellie again, who nodded.

"Oh yeah?" I said, drinking more of my pint. They giggled again and I felt intimidated but excited.

"I'll go and get us more drinks," I said, standing up.

When I returned from the bar, Ellie and Stephanie sat further apart than before.

"Why don't you sit between us?" Stephanie suggested.

I slid into the bench, between Ellie and Stephanie. Both of them put a hand on each of my legs.

I looked from one to the other and honestly got confused a couple of times about who was who. They seemed to find it hilarious that I was so baffled by it. Both women put their hands on the top of my thighs. I put one hand on each of theirs.

"You have lovely legs," Ellie said into my ear. She looked over me at Stephanie. "I can see what you mean."

Stephanie nodded enthusiastically.

"Yes!" She said, "And they look amazing with no jeans!"

Stephanie squeezed my leg, whilst Ellie continued to stroke my thigh. I put my arms around them.

I reached down and pinched each of their nipples. Both of them gasped and looked at me, then each other.

"I think we should get going soon, don't you?" Ellie said, looking at Stephanie.

"I agree," Stephanie said, "We can go for drinks tomorrow night."

I walked out of the bar with Stephanie and Ellie on either arm. We attracted a few stares: three girls looking as though they were about to hook up. None of us cared.

---

Stephanie kissed me passionately and unbuttoned my skinny jeans. She reached for my crotch and stroked my silky underwear.

"I want you," she said to me, stroking me and looking at Emily.

She pushed me down onto the bed, then pulled down my panties. She turned to face Emily.

"You can lick her first."

Ellie licked her lips and pulled my skinnies and panties completely off.

"I can't wait to taste your sweet pussy," she said.

Both of them were still in their dresses, but Stephanie kicked her sandals off as Ellie started to lick my clit.

She licked hungrily and passionately. It was almost impossible to believe that we'd just met. She hooked her tongue into my vagina, then licked my clit again. My clit throbbed in her mouth and I moaned with pleasure.

Stephanie was undressing herself beside me.

She climbed above my head and lowered her pussy onto my face. I licked her with the same eagerness Ellie did me and moaned into her wet pussy. Stephanie moaned loudly, too and ground herself into my face.

She squealed with pleasure as I licked her and I groaned and moaned into her pussy. Ellie's mouth relentlessly sucked me and she stopped and slapped my clit several times.

When she pulled her mouth away from my pussy, I expected Stephanie to climb off my face, but she didn't. I heard her and Ellie kissing and moaning together, then felt Ellie's legs straddling me.

"I want to feel your clit against mine," Ellie said, lowering her wet pussy onto mine.

I kept licking Stephanie as she rubbed herself against my mouth. "Lick me faster," she ordered, "Faster!"

I licked faster and moaned into her loudly. Ellie's warm, wet pussy was rubbing against mine and the pleasure was intense and overwhelming. I felt smothered by Ellie and Stephanie as I gave in to the pleasure they gave and received.

When Stephanie climbed off my face, I gasped to catch my breath. She looked down over me, then kissed me. The kiss was loving, passionate and even tender.

"Stephanie," I moaned to her, then, looking at Ellie, I said her name as well. "Ellie!"

Both of their brown, curly hair waved freely over their naked bodies. Their breasts were the same, C-cup size, but Ellie's nipples were larger than Stephanie's. Stephanie lowered her breast into my face and I nibbled her nipple. I licked and flicked my tongue across her, then sucked her breast.

Ellie ground against me even harder, gasping as she fucked me.

"I'm going to come," she said, "I'm going to come! Oh! Stephanie! Oh! Amanda! Stephanie!"

Ellie shouted both of our names as she came powerfully on my clit. It took all of my power not to come with her, but I wanted to save that for Stephanie.

Ellie climbed off me and sat at the bottom of the bed, looking up at me and Stephanie. Stephanie lowered her body down mine, facing Ellie.

"I want to fuck you both at the same time," Stephanie said.

She straddled me and lowered her clit towards mine. She pulled Ellie into her. As she rode me passionately, Ellie's clit touched hers too.Their clits rubbed together with the same rhythm and speed as

Stephanie's and mine. Until that moment I'd have not even thought it possible to double-fuck like that. I saw her ass bouncing in front of me and both of their brown, curly hair. I watched Ellie's hands gripping Stephanie's hair as they pleasured each other whilst Stephanie and I also fucked. As the speed increased, I knew I was about to come. Like Ellie, I moaned both of their names.

"Stephanie, Ellie! I'm going to come!"

"Come!" Stephanie ordered, "I want to feel you come!"

I came, powerfully, with Stephanie. Her and Ellie continued tribbing but her clit moved away from mine. The twinges of pleasure continued. I had spasms and shook as they continued to fuck each other on top of me.

"I'm coming!" Stephanie eventually shouted.

As she orgasmed, I felt her vagina pulsating on top of my vulva. I watched Ellie and her hug each other tightly as they shared the climax. Their breasts pushed together and their legs – almost of the same shade – entwined.

"That was amazing," we all agreed.

# Anklet and Stilettos

I was in a nightclub with a couple of my friends one evening, when a woman wearing an anklet and stilettos caught my eye. She was in her late 20s, dancing with her friends and clearly having a good time. We ended up dancing together, which was when I complimented her anklet.

"That looks very pretty," I said into her ear, pointing at the anklet during a short gap in the music. She simply smiled, put her arms around my neck and continued to dance. We danced together until the early hours of the morning, when the club started to empty.

We didn't drink a lot of alcohol, opting instead for energy drinks during the last hour or two of clubbing. I found out that her name was Melody and she was a final year student. We were both wide awake when I asked her,

"Would you like to come back to mine?"

She had nodded, silently, before going to get her jacket from the cloakroom. I watched her straight, long blond hair falling down her back, still looking perfect as she walked away from me. Her ass fitted into her tight, silver dress perfectly and she walked classily in her matching stiletto shoes. The anklet was silver, too. She looked like a beautiful fairy.

---

We shared a taxi back to my apartment and she started to talk a little more.

"Wasn't that a great night?" She said.

I nodded. "Brilliant," I said, "All the more so for meeting you!"

She smiled sweetly. Her make-up looked as though it had been freshly applied. Maybe it had, I thought. She could have touched it up in the toilets.

The journey to mine was very short and we walked out of the taxi, still chatting excitedly.

"Some of those drops, though!" She said, "The DJs were brilliant. I don't think I've ever felt so absorbed in the music!"

I agreed with her. "Absolutely," I said, "It was something else."

I opened the door to my apartment and led her into the living room.

"Nice place," she said, "Very tidy."

I smiled. I did take pride in keeping my apartment clean and tidy. You never knew when you were going to take someone back there, after all!

"Would you like a drink?" I asked her.

"Coffee, please," she said.

It was about 3.30am.

---

I went to make the coffee and Melody followed me to the kitchen. She stroked my back as I was turned to the kitchen surface. I turned to her and kissed her.

We'd kissed already, whilst dancing, but this was different. She allowed her tongue to really explore my mouth and her breathing was heavy. I pulled her in close to me and she stroked my breasts. Quickly, her hand found my pussy and she moaned as she touched it. She pushed her body further into mine and I stroked her long, blonde hair. She smelt sweet and perfumed, somehow, even after hours of clubbing.

She kissed me some more, then started to pull off my top. I moaned as she touched my nipples. Electricity seemed to come from her fingers.

She threw my top to the ground and I unzipped the back of her dress. She shook her head slightly and unzipped my tight trousers. She pulled them down, then pulled my thong down. I stood, naked from the waist down, before her.

"I love a tight, juicy pussy," she said. Her blue, innocent-looking eyes seemed incongruous with the words. I moaned and grabbed her hair again. We kissed roughly and she kept cupped my crotch, squeezing it and running her hand up and down me. I pulled at her dress again and she stepped away. She pulled off her own dress and stood before me, in a strapless black bra and a tiny black thong. The stilettos stayed on her feet, with the anklet.

She walked confidently away from me, through my apartment in her underwear and stilettos. I followed her like a dog, towards my bed. She jumped onto it and opened her legs. She pulled down her black thong and stroked her pussy.

"Mmm, I'm so wet," she said, staring at me as she rubbed herself.

I climbed onto the bed and kissed her again. My clit was throbbing as I pushed it into hers. She moaned and pushed her body further towards mine. I leant and kissed her breasts, then unhooked her bra. Naked apart from the anklet and stilettos, her body glistened and I saw the movement of her breathing.

She rubbed her own nipples and I moaned as I watched her. Our clits lightly rubbed together.

"Fuck me," she mouthed. I started to grind.

She moaned loudly and I grunted with pleasure. She moved her hips energetically and I thrust in and out of her with speed. In many ways, we were still dancing.

"Oh God," I moaned as I watched her face changing with the ecstasy she felt. Her mouth was open and her eyes were half-closed.

"Yes!" She moaned, "Oh God, yes! I love you fucking me. Yes! Fuck me! Fuck me!"

I fucked her and she fucked me back. Our bodies banged together quickly and her moans were loud and consistent. I slapped the back of her thigh and she screamed and her body shook. I did it again and she started to fuck me even faster. She reached around and put her finger right at the edge of my ass. She started to push her finger into my asshole. I gasped and yelped as she pushed her finger inside. My vision blurred and the pleasure I felt overwhelmed me. I came, violently, as her own body shook with orgasm. She gasped and ground into me, before her body bucked beneath me.

We lay in a sweaty, satisfied heap on my bed until she whispered into my ear.

"How about that coffee?"

# Tattooed Tits

It was Friday evening. I'd attended a local gig, that my friend's band were playing at and it had been pretty good. It was only 11pm, but the night was coming to an end. Some people were talking about where to go on to.

My friend who was in the band was keen to go to a rock club. I was quite happy to, especially due to the fact that he had a lot of girls around him, some of whom I sensed were gay!

"I'm in," I said to him, in ear shot of some of the girls. One of them smiled straight at me.

"Cool," she said, still looking at me. I winked at her.

---

Just one hour later, we were kissing in the corner of a dark club. Her name was Annie. The music was loud and the clientele were very drunk. We were tipsy, but not on the same level as many of the people in there.

"Where do you live?" Annie shouted into my ear. She was in her mid-20s, had black hair with a big purple streak and lots of visible tattoos.

"Not far," I said, "But I'll probably still get a taxi."

She stared at me.

"I think I'm ready to go," she said.

I understood, perfectly. We walked outside and hailed a cab.

---

In the taxi, her hand was on my thigh and mine on hers. The driver kept looking at us in the mirror, else I'd have certainly slipped my fingers up her short, black, denim skirt. She wore fishnets with holes in them and big, heavy boots. I wanted to make more holes in those fishnets.

When we got back to mine, Annie pushed me roughly onto my sofa. She jumped on top of me and kissed me passionately. I returned her kiss, pulling her body into me and wrapping her legs around my body. I was aching with desire. I longed for her to touch me. She ground into me and moaned.

I wore leather trousers. She unzipped them and pulled them down. She helped to pull off my boots, then unzipped hers. She straddled me again. I felt her fishnet tights upon my bare skin. My panties touched hers.

She ripped the fishnets around her crotch and pushed her tiny panties to the side.

She moaned with anticipation before my finger entered her, and when it did, she screamed with pleasure.

"Yes!" She said, "Fuck me! Fuck my tight cunt!"

She pulled off her black blouse and unhooked her bra. Her tattooed tits swayed on top of me and I leaned forward to lick her erect nipple. She bounced on top of me, moving her tits as she did so. I spotted a pattern of roses and a skull, plus more floral decoration on her tits.

I pushed my finger into her as she rode my hand and gasped as she rested her hands against my neck. She didn't strangle me, but left them there enough to make me feel on edge. I thrust into her faster and with more force.

She took one hand away from my neck and slapped my clit. I gasped as she continued fucking my finger. The fishnet material rubbed around my crotch but I didn't care; she looked so sexy. I stared at her thighs as they moved on me. She bounced and screamed with pleasure. She reached up to my black, short hair and grabbed it. She leant down and kissed my forehead, fucking me even more frantically. She lowered her body so that she lay on top of me and moved her hips wildly. Her tight pussy ate my fingers and she reached down to rub my clit. The pleasure was intense and amazing. I ran my hands down her bare back, then spanked her fishnet-covered ass. She screamed when I spanked her, so I did it again. The more I spanked her, the louder she screamed. She started shaking violently and digging her fingers into my neck. I spanked her again, even harder than before and she gasped and her body went rigid. She came on my fingers and I kept fucking her with them.

Her own thrusts slowed down as she came but mine sped up. She screamed and screamed and seemed out of control of her body. I fucked her even harder as she rubbed my clit. I knew that I was close to climax, myself.

I spanked her again and she screamed. She started to fuck my hand again as she fucked me with hers and I groaned loudly into her. I felt myself starting to come and I pulled her further into me.

As she lay on top of me, with our hands still touching each other's pussies, she whispered into my ear.

"I knew I wanted you."

# Hot Tub Pleasure

It's not every day that you (or I, at least!) get invited to a hot tub party. I didn't really know what to expect, when my old friend – Lisa – from college called to say she was having a gathering that he thought I'd be interested in.

She assured me that there would be lots of lesbians there, and that the general idea was that we were all going to have 'fun'.

Slightly apprehensively, I accepted his invitation. I'm so glad I did.

---

When I arrived, six people were already in the hot tub, including Lisa. I could tell that none of them were wearing any clothes, so followed their lead.

I was given a warm welcome by Lisa and all the others. Lisa told me to help myself to champagne, which was in a fridge next to the tub. I did as she said, then lowered myself into the warm, bubbly water.

"Bev, this is Amanda," Lisa said, introducing me to the woman closest to her. It wasn't clear whether or not they were together. "This is Sammy and Harriet," she gestured at two gothic-looking women in the tub, "And these are Bernard and Kate." She pointed at a straight couple.

I said hi to all of them, as I sat between Lisa and Sammy. Lisa started talking to Bev, who sat beside her, and Sammy addressed me.

"First time?" She asked. Harriet leaned over her to look at me.

"Yes," I said, looking at Sammy's breasts at the top of the water. She had cute, pink nipples that were small and pointy. Harriet's were similar, though her breasts were smaller. I looked at those, too, and wondered how the hot tub thing would work. Everyone was already naked. How did flirting happen? How were things going to progress?

"So, have you two been here before?" I asked them. They looked at each other and smiled, then turned back to me.

"Once or twice," Sammy said.

My clit was already erect under the water. I looked around the tub. Lisa and Sammy looked cosy, as did Kate and Bernard. I noticed when I looked properly at Kate and Bernard that she was stroking his cock beneath the water. She saw me looking and smiled at me. I nodded, then turned back to Sammy and Harriet. Sammy's hand was on Harriet's leg.

Unexpectedly, Kate and Bernard walked over to me in the pool.

"Hello," they said, "We've not seen you before."

I looked at the couple. They were my age and both wore wedding rings. I assumed they were married.

"It's my first time here," I said, "Lisa just invited me here yesterday."

She smiled and looked my body up and down, then looked at her husband. He nodded.

"Would you like to fuck my wife?" He asked.

I tried not to look shocked. I looked at Kate. She had a great body and she looked horny. Her nipples were erect and she was stroking her own thighs. She had dark hair and wore lots of black make-up around her eyes.

"Yes," I said, "If that's okay."

Bernard nodded at me, then at his wife. He returned to his seat, whilst Kate wrapped her legs around me.

---

Feeling the bubbles underneath my ass was strange as she straddled me and stroked my pussy.

"I've wanted to fuck you since the second you walked in here," she whispered into my ear.

I kissed her and ran my hands down her warm, wet back. I slapped her ass in the water and she moaned. She turned around to look at her husband. He was watching vividly, and masturbating. The girls to my right were kissing and Lee and Lisa were fondling each other.

I slapped Kate's ass again and watched as she bit her lip. She guided my cock into her eager, soaking pussy. I groaned as she started to grind on me.

I pushed my clit into hers from beneath as she rode me energetically. Her wet tits hit my chest and I squeezed her breasts. I slapped her ass again whilst she rode me and she screamed with pleasure. Her husband continued to masturbate whilst he watched us.

She got faster and faster as she rode me and I knew that I would come in no time at all. I spanked her harder and harder, repeatedly as she screamed into my ear. She came on my clit, then gripped me whilst she felt the intensity of the orgasm fade. She started to ride me again and I knew that I was going to come. I felt her clit throbbing against mine. Her pussy was warm and wet and she was still moaning loads from the orgasm and continued pleasure. I slapped her ass again and she moved her body from side to side, stimulating me from different angles. I came powerfully with her whilst her husband reached his own climax.

---

Soon after Kate had climbed off me, more visitors started to arrive. There were two more couples, one more solo man and four women who seemed to be friends. One of the women eyed me up immediately, prompting Lisa to turn to me.

"She's who I thought you would pair up with."

I watched as the women took off their clothes, with amazing confidence, and stepped into the pool. Despite being sensitive from just coming, I was still horny. I sat back in the tub and relaxed as the new visitors poured themselves some champagne. Lisa passed me another glass. I smiled gratefully.

I saw Lisa nod at the girl she'd pointed out to me and beckon for her to come over. She was young, slim and petite. Her breasts were perfectly proportionate to her figure and she had a tiny triangle of pubic hair.

She walked up to me confidently, with champagne in her hand.

She lowered herself into the pool beside me, then picked up her glass again.

"Cheers," she said.

We clinked glasses and I started the conversation.

"So, you know Lisa?"

"A little," she said, smiling behind me at her. She looked playfully into my eyes.

"I'm Rebecca," she said.

"Amanda," I told her.

"So, tell me about yourself." She got in there before I could.

When I mentioned that I was a security guard, Rebecca giggled with excitement.

"I've always wanted to fuck a security guard," she said bluntly. I opened my mouth in faux-shock, then laughed.

"I like how up front you are," I told her.

She shrugged, then put her hand on my thigh. I drained my champagne glass and stroked the back of her hair.

---

As we fucked, bubbles splashed around us and our faces became soaked. Rebecca was horny and frantic as she sat on top of me, facing the other way. She rubbed her whole pussy on my clit and I grabbed her breasts from behind. I looked to my side and there were more people fucking. Everybody seemed to be fucking or getting fucked. Lisa was receiving head under water.

I focused on Rebecca as her hair splashed in my face. She screamed as she bounced on top of me and I reached around to stroke her clitoris. Her scream got higher in pitch and she bounced even faster. I lifted my hips to thrust into her and moaned into her ear at the intense pleasure. I pulled her close to me and held her by hear breasts again. Her skin was smooth and wet. Her nipples were hard on her pointy breasts. I slapped her clitoris. She screamed and I slapped it again.

Suddenly, Rebecca twisted her body around and straddled me. She looked into my eyes as she rubbed her pussy against mine. She squeezed my nipples, then put her hands around my neck. She put a little pressure on as she fucked me harder and harder. I gasped and struggled to breathe as she ground on top of me. She gasped and moaned loudly as she started to orgasm on top of me. Her wet vagina was contracting in the water and the bubbles of the hot tub were stimulating us both. She screamed as she came and gripped my neck firmly with her fingers. I gasped and continued to thrust into her as she rode me even faster than before. I grabbed onto her back and pulled her close as the pleasure I felt exploded. I was gasping in the water, running my hands down her soaking back as we both slowed down our frantic fucking.

We shared a long, slow kiss before she climbed off me. She stepped out of the pool with a sensitive pussy from a powerful orgasm and picked up the bottle of champagne. She stared at me as she poured us both a glass. When she returned, we drank to celebrate the way we could make each other feel. I hugged her from the side and she patted my wet pussy.

# Punk in a Tartan Skirt

I've always had a bit of a thing for punk girls. I like their rebellious attitude, their ballsy-ness and the way they tend to be kinkier than other girls!

I was at work one day, when I met a punk in a tartan skirt.

Standing outside 'Boots', one of my usual places to be on duty, I spotted her. She ignored me as she entered the shop, then walked straight to the hair dye aisle. I watched as she picked up different colours, trying to choose between them. Eventually she settled on a dark purple dye. Her hair at the time was electric blue, so it would have been toning down, to go for the dark purple. She walked to the queue for the till. I kept watching her as she looked around the shop. She seemed fed up with the queue. She walked back to the hair dye aisle and pretended to put the box back. She slipped it into her bag.

As she walked out of the shop, she hurried past me. I followed her and quickly put my hand on her shoulder.

"You're coming with me," I said as I held her arm and led her to my small office at the end of the mall.

When we got inside, I closed the door.

"Dark purple," I said, "Subtle, for you, isn't it?"

She scowled.

"I don't want it anyway," she said, "Take it back."

She handed me the dye from her bag. There was a ring in her lip that she was playing with with her tongue. I stared at her.

"I'm afraid we can't just let this go," I said, "You have committed a crime, even by trying to steal the dye."

She sighed with frustration.

"Well, if the queue hadn't been so fucking massive, I might not have done! Those fucking slow workers. What are they getting paid for? To hold up everyone's day? And the prices, man. For a bit of purple in my hair. That I don't even want. It's fucking wrong. It's-"

"Shh." I put my finger over her mouth. She stood against the wall and I stood close next to her. She looked into my eyes and down at my finger, almost making herself go cross-eyed.

I looked down at her legs, which were covered in fishnet stockings. Her tartan skirt was short and she wore red Doc Martin's. She had a black, half-open blouse on with a skull pattern over her tit. She also wore a studded dog collar. Her electric blue hair was in a mullet style and showed off the piercings at the top of her ears.

"You a lesbian or something?" She said cockily. I smiled and pointed at the desk.

"Bend over," I instructed her.

She walked towards the desk and bent her body over it. I walked up behind her and lifted her skirt. She wore black panties, which I pulled down.

Her ass was pale and peachy. I spanked it.

"This is what happens to naughty girls," I said. I was enjoying my dominance, and her submission.

I spanked her again.

"Do you understand what you've done wrong?" I asked.

"Yes," she said. She moaned as I spanked her again. "I'm sorry, ma-am!" She said.

"Mistress," I corrected her.

I walked away as though I would stop spanking her. She stayed, bent over the desk and looked at me longingly. I could tell she wanted more of a spanking.

I approached her again and hit her hard with the palm of my hand. Her buttocks started to go red and she moaned now, unashamed to be enjoying her punishment. I hit her on both of her buttocks, one at a time but with differing gaps in between. Each spank took her by surprise.

When her ass was entirely red, I slipped my finger into her vagina. She was soaking wet. She moaned and pushed her body down into my finger. I unlocked my secret filing cabinet. There was a strapon in there.

I put on the long, hard strapon and pushed it into her. She let out a loud, satisfied moan as I the rubber cock entered her tight cunt.

"Ohhh!" She moaned as I pushed the dildo into her and thrust aggressively.

I said nothing as I fucked her hard. Her ass was bright red from the spanking and the top of my legs hit her there again and again as I fucked her hard. I grabbed the back of her bright hair and fucked her relentlessly. I spanked her again. She screamed. I reached around and squeezed her breasts and she lifted her hips to join in with my hard thrusts. I took over and fucked her even harder. She was helpless across the table as I fucked her and listened to her gasps, moans and screams of pleasure. When she came, she squirted all over the strapon and soaked my thighs. I spanked her ass again and moved the strapon around inside her. She moaned and wiggled her body on it. I pulled it out of her.

We shared an intense look as I took off the strapon. I pulled my trousers back up and she straightened our her skirt. She didn't put her panties back on.

"You may go," I told her.

We never saw each other again.

# Backstage

I was watching a goth band with a couple of my friends when I ended up on my own at the front. They'd gone to get a drink, but couldn't push their way back forward. I didn't care; I was entranced by the female bass player.

She had steady rhythm and played some excellent grooves. Unlike some of the band members, who were covered in sweat and wild with energy, she remained laid-back, whilst still looking the part and being at one with the music.

I caught her eye, halfway through the set and she looked straight at me. I felt a flutter of excitement as the music vibrated through me.

Throughout the band's set, we caught eyes several more times. When she show finished, people started to walk away from the stage, but our eyes were transfixed. She whispered something to one of the security guards, who looked at me. I nodded at him. I fantasized about switching from being security in a mall to working at concerts. He walked up to me and told me I could go with him.

I followed the guard, not worried about my disappeared friends. They had each other. He took me backstage, where the band – including the girl – were sitting with beers.

She smiled at me straight away and walked towards me.

"Hey," she said.

"Hey!" I said.

"I'm Bea," she told me.

"Amanda," I said. I was nervous and there was a lump in my throat. Something about this girl thrilled me in a way I'd never experienced before. She knew it, and stroked the side of my face.

"You looked cute, standing there all on your own," she said.

Bea had black, long hair. She wore a lot of make-up, which was even more obvious now I was up close to her. She wore a black dress with big, black boots. She had knee-high stockings on with the boots.

"That was a great show," I told her, "The music really took me... somewhere else!"

She leaned into me and kissed me. I kissed her back, conscious of the other band members in the room. She ran her hands up my back and I did the same to her. She ran her hands across my breasts. My nipples were hard. She noticed, and smiled.

We walked into a small room to the side of the main dressing room. It was private, but all it had in there was a small chair and desk. She climbed up onto the desk, pulling me into her. She sat with her legs wide and pulled my body into hers. She wrapped her legs around me as we kissed and I ran my fingers up her thighs. I found her ass and grabbed it, then reached around to her pussy. I rubbed her clitoris, which made her moan, then put my finger into her warm, wet vagina.

She moaned and ground into my finger, rhythmically, as though she were still playing music. She grabbed my ass and dug her fingers into me. She stroked my tits and pulled off my top. She unhooked my bra abd kissed my nipples, then licked me down to my torso. She undid my trousers and I hurriedly pulled them down. She pulled off her own panties and lifted her skirt all the way up. Her pussy looked so warm and inviting, I just wanted to bury my head into her. I looked into her dark eyes and saw that there was depth there. We didn't know each other at all, but we had connected through the music and were about to connect physically. She pulled my panties down and pushed her talented finger into my pussy. I moaned and fingered her back. We stimulated each other in a slow rhythm.

Although I seemed to be in control of the pace, Bea moved her hips and body naturally with me. We had a steady rhythm that was growing gradually. She moaned and held her head back as we fingered each other, obviously enjoying the pleasure she felt.

"This is so good," she moaned.

I watched her body rising and falling on the desk as I pushed my fingers in and out of her. She was beautiful, dark and gothic. She had large breasts, that were still covered by her lacy, black top. I put my hand up her top and grabbed her breast. I could feel that she had a nipple piercing. This turned me on even more and I fingered her faster.

Bea didn't seem to tired of energy as we fucked. Her body moved with mine and the speed got faster and faster.

We were fucking extremely fast, but I couldn't slow down. As I went fast, so did she. I knew that I was about to come as I gasped and looked into her eyes.

"I know" she gasped, "I'm coming!"

She came violently on my hand. I felt her pussy pulsating on my fingers. I came on hers, pushing my pussy further into her hand. We were both shaking and our bodies twitched uncontrollably. We stayed in that position for several minutes, kissing and licking each other. When I slowly pulled my fingers out of her soaking pussy, she told me:

"You can stay."

# Horny Housewife

I knew they shouldn't have, but the looks my co-workers wife gave me as I sat in their house filled me with arousal.

I'd gone there to speak to Max – my co-worker and friend – about a work-related issue we'd both been having. However, she told me that he wasn't there. She said he'd told her he was at work, then looked at me suspiciously.

I was confused; I knew he wasn't at work. I shrugged and played clueless.

"I must have got my days mixed up," I told her, unconvincingly.

The hot woman, who had introduced herself as Barbara, got up and made me a cup of tea. She was dressed in something that could have easily been a nightgown, but I think it was a dress. It was silky, red and short. She wore flip flops with it and nothing on her legs.

When she returned with the tea, I saw the outline of her nipples through the dress. She saw me noticing, smirked at me and sat next to me.

"I've always liked women," she said, looking into my eyes. The hunger was unmistakable. I looked back at her and tried to control my breathing. She had blue eyes which shone in the light of the room. Her hair was blonde and slightly wavy. Her figure was exceptional: slim but curvy, and her skin was tanned. Both her fingernails and toenails were manicured.

I knew I was already wet as she continued to sit, staring at me suggestively. I sipped the tea.

"Is the tea okay?" She asked, "Strong enough?"

I nodded.

"Perfect, thanks," I said.

She kept staring at me.

"Good," she said in a soft, sexy voice. "I like it very strong. I like to be able to taste it."

She touched my leg and I almost choked on the tea.

"Great," I said, "Me too."

Although I wanted to fuck this woman, I was worried – actually a bit scared – that Max might walk in any moment.

She stroked my thigh.

"You look good," she said, "I like your skirt."

I looked down at my skirt. I hardly ever wore a skirt. It was casual, black denim, with a button fasten.

"Thank you," I said, still looking down.

I watched her hand on my thigh. She reached further up, towards my crotch.

"I won't tell if you won't," she whispered.

---

She rubbed me through the denim of my skirt. I opened my mouth to speak, but she placed her finger above my lips.

"Shh," she said, "You don't need to say anything."

Her face got closer to mine and immediately our mouths entwined. She moaned as her tongue entered my mouth and pushed her body into me. She reached up my skirt: I wore no tights. I returned her passion with a warm kiss and reached for her breast. I squeezed it and she rubbed my clit over my panties.

"Slap my tit," she said, "Please, please, slap my titties!"

I slapped her tits lightly, still kissing her. She moaned loudly and climbed on top of me.

"You're the kind of woman I fantasize about," she said, moving her body on top of me. I watched, mesmerised by her tanned skin in the red dress. Her nipples were completely sticking out and seemed to have grown even bigger. I slapped her tits again. She squealed and moved her body from side to side.

Barbara reached down and pulled at my skirt. It fell onto the floor. She tugged my pink panties down and stroked my thighs again.

"Mmm," she said, leaning down towards my pussy, "I can't wait to taste your sweet pussy."

She licked me with relish, kissing my clit and spitting on me before using her whole tongue to pleasure me.

I moaned loudly as she moved her tongue around. The sensations were overwhelming. She was unpredictable in her next moves. I never knew what was coming next. She delighted me every second.

I gasped and moaned as she licked me, bringing me closer and closer to orgasm. When my clit got extremely hard in her mouth, just as I was about to come, she pulled her mouth away.

She stood in front of me and took off the red dress. She had no underwear on at all. She reached down to her pussy and started to rub it in front of me. I reached out for her and grabbed her ass. It was smooth and firm. I spanked it softly and she squealed.

She jumped on top of me and lowered herself down onto me.

"I want my clit to fuck yours," she said seriously.

I nodded and thrust into her as we rubbed our soaking wet pussies against each other. We both moaned and started to thrust together. We were frantic from the beginning, fucking each other as though it were the most important thing in the World. It was, to us.

I rubbed against quickly and powerfully and she pushed herself into me, screaming as the pleasure grew increasingly intense.

I gripped onto her blonde hair and watched as her face distorted as she got closer to orgasm. She bit on her bottom lip and her eyes closed slightly, so I could only see the whites. Her moans got louder and louder and higher and higher, then her fingers gripped my chest.

"FUCK!" She shouted, "FUCK! YES!"

She fucked me even faster as she screamed the word, "FUCK!" And I felt her coming on top of me. She pushed into me even harder and our clits throbbed as she came, screaming, "FUCK! FUCK! FUCK!"

I pulled her body into mine and rubbed her tits against me as we continued to move together. She slowed down as she orgasmed but I kept the pace, making her scream even more.

I felt the entire lower half of my body pleasurably tensing ready for the ultimate release. My clit got even more rigid and so did my legs. It was almost as

though I turned to stone before I finally screamed
with Barbara:


"FUCK! YES!"

# Sabrina in Stockings

Who can resist a woman in stockings? Not me, that's for sure. When I met Sabrina, I knew she had it in her to blow any man or woman's mind. I wanted to blow hers.

We were introduced via a mutual friend, who was also female. Perhaps strangely, the friend was an ex-lover. But let's not go into that right now. This story is about Sabrina. Sabrina, Sabrina!

Our first date was a picnic in a beautiful park. I'd suggested that we go for a walk together and had provided a picnic basket filled with food for us to enjoy. We ate small sandwiches – that I'd even cut into triangles – as well as white wine and fruits. Sabrina wore no stockings this day, but a pretty, summer dress with flip flops.

She invited me to her apartment the following day. She wanted to cook for me. It took all of my willpower to not physically jump with joy.

---

Sabrina's flat was small, clean and tidy. There were paintings on the wall of abstract, bright art and she burned incense sticks. We sat together on her fabric sofa that was covered with a bright throw. We drank bottled beer.

"I must admit," she said, "When I insisted on cooking for you this evening, it was more because I wanted to see you, and do something nice for you... I mean, I'm not an exceptional cook."

I laughed and shook my head. She looked stunning and cute as she spoke to me. She wore short, blue denim shorts and hold-up stockings. She wore no shoes. On her top half, was a black, low-cut t shirt. She looked effortlessly sexy. She wore her dark hair down and it flowed over her back and on top of her breasts. Her eyes were made up with dark make-up and she wore red lipstick. She had a tiny piercing in her nose. She sipped again at her beer, looking at me expectantly.

"Well," I said, "I must admit that when I excitedly agreed, it was more to do with seeing you than eating whatever you might cook!"

She laughed. I couldn't tell whether she was relaxed or nervous.

"I'm glad," she said, standing up. "I've cooked us a Chilli Con Carne, anyway. Vegetarian."

I licked my lips comically. She laughed again.

"I can't wait," I said, "Thank you."

She smiled at me softly, then walked to the kitchen.

---

When she returned, she approached her stereo.

"The food will be ready any time," she said, "But let's wait until later, yeah?"

I nodded.

"Sure," I said. I couldn't help but stare at her legs. The stockings came up to just under where her short denim shorts ended. Surely she must know how sexy she looked? There was a small patch of bare thigh above the stocking that I couldn't take my eyes off. I ached with longing as I imagined pulling her shorts down.

She turned around and I watched her ass. It fit perfectly into the shorts, as though they were made just for her. She bent over and I felt myself shudder with desire.  I imagined spanking her.

She pressed play on the stereo. Strange, Indian-sounding music came on.

"I love this stuff," she said, "I know it's not what you hear every day but it's so relaxing. It really makes you feel good."

I listened to the sound of sitars, droning and couldn't hide my frown.

She laughed at me again.

"Give it a chance!" She said. "Trust me!"

I shrugged my shoulders and laughed.

"Okay," I said, "It's your rules!"

She came to sit by me on the sofa, closer than she had before.

---

Our first kiss was soft, loving and playful. Our lips brushed lightly against each other and the tips of our tongues touched. I opened my eyes and Sabrina opened hers, whilst we looked at each other. We were getting to know each other, I thought. We were properly learning about one another. We kissed again, this time with more intensity.

Sabrina's tongue entered my mouth as I stroked her thigh. I felt the silky stocking beneath my hand, and the frilled pattern at the top of the stocking. I touched the bare skin between the top of her right stocking and the edge of her shorts. My clit tingled.

Sabrina's skin was warm and her breathing was slow and relaxed. The music seemed to be building but it wasn't changing much. Her breath was in time with the music. I watched Sabrina's chest as it moved, dancing with the sounds from the stereo. I kissed the top of her chest, then slowly pulled off her top.

Sabrina wore a dark bra beneath the low cut top, which I unhooked, also slowly. Something told me that we were not in a rush and that the moments would be better if they were savoured. I kissed her bare, C-cup breast. She moaned quietly. I flicked my tongue across her nipple, feeling as it became erect. She held onto the back of my head, then stroked the back of my neck.

Sabrina's fingers ran down my back, then up the back of my top. She unhooked my bra, then stroked my bare skin, filling me with electricity. I looked up at her face again and kissed her lips. Each kiss seemed to get more intense. She pulled my top off of me, then pulled my bra down my arm. She kissed my breasts, licking my hard nipples. She licked down my torso and unbuttoned my black trousers.

I pulled her on top of me and unbuttoned her tiny shorts. She helped me get her out of them, then sat on me in her stockings and a small, pink thong. I stroked the front of her thong. I could feel her tiny, hard clitoris beneath my hand. She moaned and wriggled on me.

I pulled down the thong. She had a tiny strip of pubic hair, leading to a smooth vulva. I stroked her vulva. She moaned again and pulled my face into hers. We kissed some more as I rubbed around her vagina. She was soaking wet. I stroked her clitoris, then stuck my finger into her warm pussy. She gasped and reached down to rub my pussy.

She rubbed my clit with her hand and pushed her fingers into my pussy. She smiled as she kissed me and I felt the shape of her mouth moving with mine. She pulled down my panties and I kicked off my small socks. She still wore her stockings.

I stroked up and down her thighs, feeling where the stockings ended and the bare skin began. I slapped her ass gently, then guided my fingers to the entrance of her anus. She tickled my clit with her fingers, then rubbed it again. She stroked me softly and kissed me with passion.

I ran my hand back towards her vagina. She moaned louder, then, as I pushed two fingers inside her. I penetrated her with my fingers and she pushed two fingers into me.

I pulled my fingers out of her and looked into her eyes. Maintaining eye contact, I pushed three fingers into her begging vagina. She gasped loudly and closed her eyes.

Sabrina and I made love with a steady, building rhythm. The Indian music was still playing and we seemed to be making love *with* it. As more layers were introduced to the music, our sex gained a new layer of intensity. Her fingers gripped my neck, then stroked behind my ears. The top of her ass pushed down onto my hand as her pussy ate my thrusting fingers. We were steady, gentle, but absolutely intense. The music grew louder and our fingering grew deeper. The speed of the music started to increase, as did ours. We fucked together, united by our pleasure and shared rhythm. We got faster, faster, even faster.

I gasped and gripped onto her hair as the pleasure overtook my consciousness. The music got even faster. We fucked faster and her body began to buck. Mine bucked, too. We gave in to the pleasure. I pushed my hand firmly onto her clit and stimulated her powerfully. As I screamed with orgasm, her juices covered my hand. She was screaming, too.The music started to die down; to give way to a new piece. She kissed my neck gently and climbed off of me. She said nothing as her smiling eyes stared into mine. She walked back to the kitchen. I stared at her stocking-covered legs.

## Naughty Nina

I was locking up the mall one day, when a woman in her late twenties walked past me. She turned to look at me and I stared back at her, wondering where I recognised her from.

"Oh, God," she said as she saw me, "Look who it is!"

She was alone, but she seemed as though she were addressing somebody other than me. I looked around. She was talking to me.

"I'm sorry," I said, "Where do I know you from again?"

The woman's face lit up into a huge grin. She laughed out loud and I recognised the sound of her laugh. It was then that I knew where I recognised her from. I'd detained her two days previously. She'd been trying to steal a pair of boots. When I'd let her go with a warning (she'd been extremely unsuccessful in her theft attempt), she'd laughed as she walked away.

"Oh," I said as I realised. I continued walking towards the pub. I'd decided I was going to have a pint that evening, on the way home.

---

I walked into 'The Old Crown' and headed straight to the bar. I'd almost forgotten about the woman by then, until I turned around and saw her behind me. I frowned.

"Are you following me?"

There was something about the woman that unsettled me. She seemed to find everything hilarious, in a mocking way. She laughed again.

"I've just come in here for a drink," she said.

I turned around and ordered my own pint. My heart was racing.

---

As I sat at the bar, pretending to read a magazine as I sipped my lager, I couldn't help but be aware of her sitting, alone on the table behind me. Not many women did that, I thought. I turned to look at her. Like me, she was pretending to read. Or perhaps she was reading. There was a magazine in front of her and her brow furrowed as she looked down at it. She had  a glass of large, red wine that beautifully matched both her dress and her painted nails. She had straight, black hair and, despite the furrowed brow, she still smiled. She looked up at me.

"Don't worry," she said cheekily, "I'm not trying to nick anything."

I laughed nervously and turned back to my pint and magazine. I looked down and noticed that my hands were shaking.

After several minutes, she stood beside me at the bar. She was about to order another drink. Without thinking, I turned to her.

"I'll get this," I said, "If you like."

She beamed at me.

"Wow," she said, "You're too kind. Thanks. In that case, I'll have a double Bacardi and coke."

I smiled and nodded at the bartender. I ordered us both a double Bacardi and coke, then turned to her table.

"What are you reading?" I asked her.

"I'm not," she said, tossing the magazine to one side.

We both sat at the table..

---

Three Bacardi and cokes later, we are walking back to my apartment. We're both tipsy, linking arms and giggling.

"I thought you were a right bitch, when you came up to me in the store," she said, laughing. "You're actually alright, though, aren't you?"

"I can't say I thought that much of you, failing so spectacularly in your efforts to steal boots!"

"Maybe I just wanted attention."

Our eyes locked and we kissed on the street. I held on to her faux-leather jacked and her hand touched my breast. We continued walking.

---

Inside my apartment, Nina took off her tall, black boots whilst I unlaced my Doc Martins. She wore panty-hose beneath her dark red dress. She wore a statement necklace with a large heart detail.

Before I could ask her if she'd like another drink, or some food, she pounced on me. She pushed me down onto my own sofa and wrapped her legs around me.

We kissed urgently and she ran her fingers through my hair. She pulled my face towards hers and unbuttoned my uniform. She took my blouse off and stroked my tits hungrily. She almost growled as she unbuttoned my trousers. She slapped my pussy, then reached around to unzip her dress. She pulled it off and I pulled her panty-hose. She had amazingly smooth legs. I pulled the panty-hose completely off them and admired her dark red toenails. She wore a black, small thong. I hooked my finger over the side of it and pulled it down. She had a smooth, shaven pussy. I kissed her warm pussy and she pushed her crotch further into my face.

I licked around her vagina, then flicked my tongue around her anal hole. I licked the bottom of her pale buttocks, inhaling the scent of her vagina before I licked her there again. I stuck my tongue inside her and heard her moan. She grabbed the back of my head and pulled me into her.

I licked around her vagina then stimulated her clitoris with my tongue. She moaned even louder and gasped as she pushed herself into me again. Her legs wrapped around my head, then she pulled herself away from my face.

"I need to fuck you," she said, "Do you have any toys?"

I ran to my room to grab a double-ended dildo. I didn't use them often, but it was essential; it would be just right for this woman.

When I returned, I stared at her beautiful, bare body. She had a slim figure with small but perky boobs and a tight ass. Her necklace was still around her neck, but wonky. Her black hair fell down her back.

I held the dildo in front of me.

"Let's fuck," I said.

I walked back to the sofa and put it in front of my crotch. She climbed on top of me again and lowered herself onto the rubber dildo. She gasped and pushed the other end into me. I gasped as the rubber cock penetrated me. She moved her pelvis and hips as she bounced on top of me. Our bodies moved together as we fucked each other with the rubber cock. She moaned loudly with pleasure and moved in circular motions on top of my body. I watched her in amazement as I felt the pleasure growing. She kept moaning. I heard myself moaning, too. Her pale, slim body moved on top of me and her smile got wider. With her mouth open, she licked her lips then screamed. She fucked me faster. She reached around and grabbed my ass as she fucked me. I leant into her breasts and bit her nipples. She screamed again. I kissed her neck then sucked on her warm skin as she rode me. Our breasts pushed together. She got quicker and quicker and gripped onto my hair then spanked my ass again. I screamed and took control of the thrusting. I pushed in and out of her as fast as I could and gasped into her neck as I felt myself coming close to orgasm. She screamed into my ear and I felt the throbbing of her clit on mine. Her vagina began to throb and she let out a prolonged scream. I knew she was coming. I fucked her even faster and allowed myself to release. My pleasure peaked as I held her close to me, feeling her heart pounding into mine.

"Amanda," she moaned into my ear, "You hot bitch."

# The Librarian

As a keen writer, I do, of course, also like to read. It might sound as though I spend all of my time having sex with beautiful women but these are just extracts from years of experience.

Of course, I'm not about to share a story about one of my encounters with a book. Much better than that; my dreams came true one day when I hooked up with a sexy librarian!

---

Rebecca was older than me, but she looked great for it. She had blonde hair, that she always wore tied back with a large clip. She wore glasses and dressed in a smart, well-fitted grey suit. She wore high heels to work and you could hear her every time she walked through the library. Her make-up style was subtle but noticeable and she often looked up from

145

behind her desk to see men staring at her. She always took it on the chin. I suspected that, despite her apparent 'geekiness', she was pretty hard.

I was checking out a Charles Bukowski book one day, when she spoke to me with delight.

"Bukowski! Cool. I love Charles Bukowski. I read his book, 'Post Office', in just one hour! It's brilliant!"

I nodded enthusiastically. Partly excited that she was talking to me and partly genuinely keen on the author.

"He's great, isn't he," I said, "So authentic, so easy to read!"

She agreed.

"Do you like his poetry?" She asked.

I nodded. "What I've read of it, yes!" I said, "I like The Bluebird!"

"That's my favourite!" The librarian had said. We were grinning at each other like fools when she looked at her watch.

"You're just in time, actually," she said, "We're closing now!"

"I know," I said, "I've just finished work. I'm glad I made it on time."

She looked at my security uniform.

"It's good to know that the book's in safe hands," she said.

She handed me the book, stamped with my return date and looked at the door. She started to walk around the library, telling people that it was time to leave. I stood there, still. I was aware that it looked strange, but I wanted to talk to her some more. She seemed keen. I wasn't going to miss a chance like that.

---

When she saw me again, she looked a little confused.

"I'm sorry," she said to me, "Can I help you with something else?"

I took a deep breath.

"Well," I said, "I know you probably get offers like this all the time, possibly from all kinds of creeps. Your instant reaction might be to decline, but would you like to go for a drink? We can talk about Bukowski, some more."

She smiled at me and looked around. The last couple of people were leaving the library.

"I just have a couple of things to do," she said, looking at her desk and a pile of books, "But yes. And I don't get asked all the time. Most people seem to be scared of me."

I laughed and looked at the books.

"Would you like a hand?" I asked.

She shook her head.

"No, thank you," she said. "I'll meet you in the cocktail bar, two doors down, in ten minutes?"

I held my book in the air with elation.

"See you there!" I said, "What's your drink?"

"Get me something you think Bukowski would approve of," she laughed, walking away from me. Her ass fit perfectly into her grey suit. I walked away with a hard on in my trousers.

---

I walked to the cocktail bar and stared at the list. Bukowski would have approved of any one of them, I thought, laughing to myself. As long as the alcohol content was high! In the end, I ordered us both a long island ice tea. As I waited for them to be poured, I looked around the building.

It was only 6pm, so it wasn't overly busy. There were a few after-work drinkers in there, but many of them were just having one and leaving. These kind of places, I knew from experience, didn't get busy until 8 or 9 o' clock. I was pleasantly surprised when I paid for the drinks and found out that they were two for one. It was happy hour until 7pm.

I sat with the two cocktails on a small table on a comfortable leather sofa. There were two chairs the other side of the table, but I'd put Rebecca's drink next to me, hoping she'd sit by me on the sofa.

When she walked in the building she smiled at the bartender first.

"Hey, Jim!" She said.

My heart sank. Jim blew her a kiss and winked. She laughed, then turned to me. *What if she was really, 100% straight?*

"Hey," she said.

My spirits immediately lifted again.

She came and sat next to me on the sofa, as I'd wished for, then looked approvingly at the cocktail.

"Long Island?" She asked.

I nodded. "Yep," I said, "Reckon Charles would approve?"

She laughed. "Of course," she said, "The combination of alcohols in here would be enough to get even him quickly battered."

We said cheers and sipped our drinks. Then started to talk.

---

Conversation flowed freely with Rebecca. We talked about a variety of books, from the classics all the way through to Irvine Welsh. She was an interesting character with an intriguing rebellious side that was brought to life through the books she read. When she invited me to her apartment to see her personal library, I couldn't believe my luck.

---

Rebecca's apartment was spacious and modern. She had a large living room, with no TV in there. There were three book cases. I had expected them to be neatly ordered, with her being a librarian, but the filing seemed to be completely random. There was a Plato book next to a Haruki Murakami novel. Next to both of those, was a biography of Keith Richards.

"This is the most random book case I've ever seen," I told her, laughing, "I was expecting it to be neat and in chronological, alphabetical, colour coded order!"

She laughed.

"I like to escape when I'm at home," she said, "Besides, the randomness inspires creativity."

I nodded thoughtfully, imagining how combining Keith Richards with Haruki Murakami and Plato could encourage an extremely original thought.

She looked at me playfully.

"But you didn't just come here to look at my books, did you?" She said.

I shook my head. We stood by her bookcase looking into each other's eyes. Hers were dark and thoughtful. Her eyebrows were thin and plucked and her face rested in a faint smile. She smirked at me gently.

"Come on," she whispered, "I'll show you my bedroom."

---

I followed Rebecca into her bedroom as she threw her blazer onto her chair. I unbuttoned my top two buttons. She turned to me and pushed me onto her bed. She had purple bed sheets that were neatly made. We kissed lovingly and she stroked the front of my shirt, teasing my nipples.

She stood over me, unbuttoning her blouse. She wore a purple, lacy bra. I reached out and cupped her breasts, kissing them one by one. I unhooked her bra and she let it fall down her arms. I kissed her breasts again, running my tongue over her nipples, one by one.

Rebecca fell onto me on her bed and we both lay down. I ran my hand down the side of her body and unbuttoned her grey trousers. She slid out of them with my help and took of her shoes in an instant.. Just in a purple, lacy pair of knickers, she watched as I pulled off my blouse. She reached around and unhooked my bra. She leaned down and kissed my nipples tenderly, one by one. I moaned and then kicked off my shoes. I pulled off my trousers and panties becoming naked with her. She reached for my pussy and stroked it as she kissed me again. I hooked my thumb into her panties and pulled them down.

155

She had a neat patch of pubic hair. I touched her vulva and she moaned into my mouth.

"I knew you were hot the moment I saw you," she whispered to me.

I rolled onto my back and pulled her on top of me. She straddled me as we kissed again. I reached for a hair clip, but she took over, removing it carefully so that her hair fell free. She kissed me again. Her breasts pushed into mine. I felt her nipples hard close to mine. My clit was aching. I moaned with anticipation as I kissed her. Her breathing was heavy. She reached down for my clit and stroked it.

"I have something," she whispered.

She opened her bedside-draw and pulled out a strap-on. She tied it around her front.

"You need to be fucked," she said.

She was right. I really, really needed to be fucked. I stared at her breasts as she slowly, gently but with desire pushed the strap-on inside me.

She moaned loudly as she lowered herself completely onto me, touching my clit with hers as the strap-on penetrated me. I screamed and pushed my pelvis up into her. She stimulated me deep inside. I reached around and held onto her buttocks as I joined in with her thrusts. I watched her breasts moving as we fucked and her blonde hair bouncing around her shoulders.

"Oh! God!" She moaned as we fucked. She fell down onto me so that her face was next to mine. She kissed my neck and I kissed hers back. Our fucking was steady but the thrusts were all deep. We moaned as each one reached its full depth. I started to push myself into her faster and move my clit against hers. She ground onto me some more. Her legs moved and her hips did circular motions. She bit my neck and I winced with shock. She sunk her teeth in as she kept fucking me. She was in control. She lifted her body up and looked down at me as she fucked me urgently.

She squeezed my nipples, then left her hands flat on my chest as she pushed up and down on me. I watched as she orgasmed on top of me, her body shaking and her face relaxing into a smile that looked almost like laughter. She moaned loudly as she came and continued to thrust quickly into me. I too was about to climax. I squeezed her ass hard as I exploded with the strap-on inside me. I didn't realise until my orgasm was over that I'd moaned loudly throughout the several seconds of total euphoria. She leant down and kissed me again. Her clit still throbbed on top of mine.

# Book Club Heat

So, I have to confess, it was finding out just how hot bookish women were that inspired me to join a book club. It wasn't my usual scene but, as I said, I do love to read.

The first session I attended was in a function room at a local pub. The book we were going to talk about was a new novel by McEwan: 'Machines Like Me'. I had really enjoyed the book and I was excited to be discussing it with others. But, who am I kidding, I was hoping to meet a hot woman there.

When I arrived, I was excited to see a table of 12 people; mostly women. I smiled at them all and took my seat. One of the 4 other men in the room nodded at me, then looked at me suspiciously. I smiled at him. I was no longer in my security gear but I still looked tough, which could intimidate some people. He looked away and I was greeted by the book club chairwoman.

"You must be Amanda?" She said, "Thanks for the email, and your attendance! We're delighted that you could join us today."

"Thank you," I said, "I'm assuming you're Sarah?"

She smiled and blushed a little.

"Yes," She said, "That's right."

I glanced at her hand. She wore a wedding ring.

Sarah introduced me quickly to the others in the room. I instantly forgot most of their names but there was one woman – Lisa – who was unforgettable. She was mid-20s, cute and nerdy-looking, with tattoos on her arms. She had a frog on her wrist and a large passage of text covering the inside of her arm. Her hair was ginger, quite short and styled with a headband. She wore a vintage blouse and skinny jeans, with Converse trainers. My mouth went dry when I looked at her and I sensed that she was the reason I was there.

Quickly, we settled into book club and some people had some quite interesting ideas about the book. I stayed pretty quiet, besides pointing out the elegance and humanity in McEwan's writing. Lisa made quite a lengthy monologue.

She discussed the bravery of the setting of the book, and how much effort that must have taken on the author's part. She laughed out loud at some of the things the robot said and wrote in the book, then reflected on how AI can never produce works of beauty. She talked about the characters as though they were friends she'd known and thought about for years. She was a wonderful, thoughtful, beautiful woman.

---

As we were already in a pub, it was easy to buy Lisa a drink after book club. She drank pints of lager, which caused one or two raised eyebrows from a couple of men in the group. We both laughed about this. Like me, she didn't care. We talked about her philosophical insights and she revealed to me that she was an avid reader who always liked to reflect on a deeper level. She felt that to read a book for entertainment was an offence to the novelist and the novel. She was intense.

She drank extremely quickly but I matched her pace. Others started to leave. We were alone together in the pub within the hour. We got on extremely well.

Closing time came too soon and I worried that she would like to leave. I almost fell with shock when she said to me,

"I live upstairs. Would you like to come up?"

---

*She lives upstairs*, I remember thinking, *why didn't she say? This is amazing! Upstairs!*

Her small apartment above the pub was aged but clean. There were an abundance of books, many of which weren't even on shelves. She had a small television and a stereo. There were notebooks of her own writing scattered on the coffee table.

She gestured at her small leather sofa.

"Take a seat," she said, "I'll make us a drink."

I sat down as she went and fixed us both a large gin and tonic, with frozen fruit in it.

"I know it's a bit summery," she laughed, "But I don't have much else. I can't possibly stomach any more beer!"

"Me neither!" I lied. I drank the gin and tonic. It was actually fantastically refreshing. I smiled at Lisa.

"Thanks for inviting me up," I said.

"My pleasure," she said, "Music?"

I nodded, "Yes, that would be great."

She walked over to the stereo and put on The Cure. I smiled and leant back. The music reminded me of ten years previous. I felt free and high.

I watched as Lisa walked back towards me. She took off her headband and shook her ginger hair. She kicked off her converse.

"Time to chill!" She said.

She came and sat by me and I put my arm around her. Before the second song had come on the stereo, we were kissing.

---

We kissed without inhibition. Our lips danced together with the sound of The Cure and our hands wandered freely. We removed each other's clothes effortlessly and were already naked before she led me into her bedroom. I followed her like a dog, gazing in awe at her pale buttocks and long legs.

Lisa lay back on her bed and pulled me with her. The bed was clean and fresh with a pastel pattern. We kissed some more, with the same easy, natural feeling. My finger entered her vagina. She moaned beautifully. I licked her thighs and further up until my tongue found her clit. I felt her legs tighten against my face as I licked her. She moaned softly and moved her body as I stimulated her with my tongue. When she started to tense, I stopped licking her and kissed up her body. We kissed again and she reached down for my clit. We both moaned as she pulled me on top of her.

I thrust into her, rubbing my clit against hers and looked down at her body. Her tiny, pink nipples were pointy and hard. Her leg hooked around the back of me as she joined in with my thrusts. We fucked each other in a steady rhythm and held each other close. I kissed her cheek, then she turned to kiss me again. We shared a long, passionate kiss as we fucked, moaning into each other's mouths.

I pulled my face away and fucked her faster. She closed her eyes and thrust into me. She moaned loudly and continuously as we bounced together. Suddenly, Lisa sat up and I pulled her onto me. She put her hands behind her back and fucked me using all her strength. I held her around her waist and watched as she fucked me. Her ass was bashing against me and she rode me with enthusiasm and vigour. I pushed her backwards, then instructed her,

"Get on all fours."

She got on her hands and knees and I spanked her ass. I reached around and teased her clit and she moaned and tried to push herself into my hand.. I teased her some more, stroking her gently and spanking her softly.

"Oh God," she moaned deeply, "Please, oh God."

I teased her some more. I took my hand away then stroked around her pussy again. She tried to push but I left my fingers right at the entry to her pussy. Moving them slightly. Suddenly, I pushed them into her again. She screamed as I fucked her with my hand. I reached around and rubbed her clit with my other hand. I saw her tits wobbling beneath her as I pleasured her. I pulled away from her clit and spanked her ass again and she dug her fingers into the pillow. Her body dropped a little and her face went into the pillow.

"Yes! Yes!" She screamed into the pillow. "Oh my GOD!"

I rubbed her clit again. Her body was shaking and her fingers were firmly gripping the pillow her face was pressed into. I kept rubbing and fingering her harder and harder and I knew that she was close to coming. She screamed loudly into the pillow and I felt her pussy spasming on my had. She was contracting and pulsating as she screamed and her body was shaking violently.

"I'M COMING!" She screamed.

# 30 Lashes

I lay, face-down with my arms bound together above my head. They were also attached, firmly, to the bench I lay on. My legs were trying to kick but they also couldn't move. They were tied together with rope and attached to the bench also. It was a good job I trusted her.

I felt cold metal scraping my back.

"This journey," her soft voice said, "That might venture further than you've been before."

She was silent for a while. In this time, the sensation I'd just felt on my back seemed to reverberate. Although I knew she was no longer stroking me with the device, I felt the sensation almost as clearly as if it were still happening.

"Are you ready?" Asked her voice from across the room.

"Yes, mistress," I answered timidly.

I heard her high-heeled boots walking across the room. They got further away from me, then started to get closer. My heart raced as the steps became close to me. The steps stopped and I knew she was next to me. I was blindfolded, so couldn't turn to look, even if that would have been permitted.

I felt a different sensation. This time it felt like leather. Again, it was reasonably cool but not compared to the metal. She stroked my bare buttocks with the leather. I felt them trembling

She struck me.

"Number 1," she said. I knew that I were getting 30 lashings that day. It was my 30th birthday.

She walked away again. It felt like forever. Like before, I focused on the sensation she'd just inflicted. Although the impact had vanished as soon as it had appeared, the sensation seemed to continue. I longed for more.

The footsteps got closer again, but she was teasing me. She walked around me several times. She laughed, mocking me, then stepped away. I heard the footsteps again but couldn't tell whether she was walking away, closer to me or even walking on the spot. My body tried to move again, but failed.

"Number 2," she barked as she cracked the whip down onto me. I wince and gritted my teeth. That one really hurt. It felt as though she'd torn my ass in two. She laughed again.

"Number 3," she said as she brought the whip down again, this time on my other buttock. They were both stinging intensely. I heard those high-heeled footsteps again.

She returned and stroked my buttocks with her gloved hand. She wore black, leather gloves. The sensation felt both soothing and sexy against my skin. I felt my buttocks trembling again. My pussy was wet and my clit was hard.

"Number 4," she said, hitting me hard with a paddle. Before I could process the sensation, she struck again.

"5, 6, 7!" She said, hitting me three times quickly. I gasped and lifted my head a little. I quickly put it back down into the bench. She tutted at me and clipped me lightly on the back of my head.

I breathed deeply and listened to her footsteps as she walked around the room some more. I imagined how she looked: dressed in black leather with her thigh-high boots. She was tall, dark and stern-looking. I wondered what she had in her hand. A whip? Another paddle? A flogger?

She was close to me again, waiting for the right time to strike.

"Amanda," she said.

"Yes, mistress," I asked. My voice shook with anticipation.

"Number 8," she said calmly. She hit me hard with a wooden cane. I screamed into the bench.

"Naughty girl," she said, standing very still over me. The stinging was overwhelming and I could focus on nothing else. It started to cease, slowly, but the pain kept throbbing. As I focused on steadying my breath, I wondered if I could really handle 22 more of these lashes.

"9, 10!" She said, hitting me two more times with the cane.

I felt a tear run down my face. My heart was beating an an alarming rate and my whole body was shaking.

*I'm a third of the way there*, I told myself, *I can do it. I can endure this.*

The sound of the heels continued. Again, I didn't know what she would strike me with next. My ass throbbed and stung like Hell.

"Number 11," she eventually said, bringing a flogger down onto the top of my thigh. My leg tried to move in reflex again, but still it remained tied down.

"12," she said, striking the same place again.

"13, 14, 15," she said, hitting me three times with the flogger: twice on the back of my thighs and once on my burning ass.

"Mistress!" I moaned. I couldn't help it.

She leant down to me.

"Yes, little girl?" She asked.

I felt many tears falling down my face.

"Thank you," I said.

She patted my head affectionately.

My mistress walked again.

*I'm half way there*, I told myself, *half way. Stay strong.*

I steadied my breathing again as I waited for her next move. There was no way of knowing what it could be, not with my mistress.

She stroked my ass with her gloved hand again.

"Very pretty," she said, "Pinks and reds."

I imagined how my ass would look. Raw, I guessed.

"There's no purple yet, though," she said.

I felt scared. She was capable of inflicting enormous amounts of pain. I thought I'd already been through the worst of it. I was wrong.

"Number 16!" She said loudly. I heard a mighty whip crack, followed by an extreme thump on my ass. It was extremely painful, cutting deep into me.

"I've drawn blood," she said, unapologetically.

My eyes were streaming and my heart was pounding. My hands were shaking together.

"17" She shouted. Again, I heard the loud crack of the whip, then felt the extreme, multi-sensational pain.

"NO!" I shouted. I heard her put down the whip.

She leant down and whispered in my ear.

"Would you like me to stop?"

I shook my head.

"You know the safe word."

I shook my head again.

She patted my head and gripped onto my hair.

"Good girl."

The tears stopped falling as she walked around the room. The pain started to subside. I felt floaty and free, but the anticipation of what she would do next was still strong. I wondered again whether I would make it to 30. I reduced my aim, privately, to 20.

"18," she said. She hit me with a large paddle. It covered both of my buttocks simultaneously. It felt like a sharp thump, but on my already tender ass it was overwhelming.

"19, 20, 21," she said, hitting me three times.

"22, 23," she said, hitting me twice more.

She stopped again. I lay there letting the pain sink in. It was beginning to feel less like pain and more like pleasure. This was what I'd been chasing.

She walked around again and I craved her strongly as I heard her heels. On other days, I might have been cheeky, asking, "Please, Mistress! Hurry!" This would usually get me in trouble (meaning more spankings!). However, on this occasion, I waited, patiently.

"Number..." She said, dragging her sentence out deliberately, "24."

I felt something new hit my ass. Something I hadn't felt before. It was sharp and cold. It felt like metal. Perhaps what she'd stroked me with before.

"25," she said, hitting me with the same thing again. The pain was shocking and I felt like I might pass out.

She paused again after the 25th strike. The pain in my ass was throbbing and my face was soaked with tears.

I thought about calling the safe word, but only momentarily. As soon as I imagined the lashes actually ending, I changed my mind about wanting it.

Those footsteps again. My cock throbbed at the image of her in my mind. I heard the sound of a flogger running through the air, but it sounded strange. It sounded as though there were two floggers, moving at slightly different times, I thought.

I could tell by the sound of her shoes that she was next to me again.

Expecting a strike, I flinched as she touched me. But she was stroking me. She ran, as I had thought, two floggers across my bare back.

Anticipating her strike, I winced again. She laughed.

"It's just a little stroking," she said, "Surely that doesn't hurt too badly, little boy?"

I said nothing as I waited. I knew that it wouldn't be long.

The floggers left my back and my mistress went silent. I heard the sound of both floggers going up in the air.

"26 and 27," she said, bringing them both down on me. One hit my left buttock and one hit the bottom of the right hand side of my back.

"28 and 29," she said, doing the same again. This time one flogger hit each buttock. I gritted my teeth and groaned into the bench. My buttocks were throbbing with pain. I couldn't take any more. *One more*, I told myself. I steadied my breathing again and thought about how my mistress would look right now, smiling over my red ass. She stroked my sore buttocks again with her leather gloves. Her gloves went up my back, then back down again, resting once more on my sore buttocks. She lifted one of them off, keeping the other in place. I heard her pick something up, but I wasn't sure what. I waited patiently. I knew that this was near the end. Number 30. I heard her put down whatever she'd picked up.

"Number 30," she whispered quietly, before spanking me hard with her leather glove.

I sighed with relief. It hadn't been as painful as a lot of her other strikes. I felt euphoric. My heart raced with mixed emotions as I felt my mistress kneeling down next to me. I felt her breath on my ear, then she asked,

"Would the birthday girl like a little extra?"

# Daring Dominance

I've always been open-minded. When it comes to BDSM, if I'm with a kinky woman, I'm happy to switch between submissive and dominant.

It was with one, extremely submissive woman that I really discovered just how dominant I could be.

---

She lay, submissively on her back before I'd even restrained her. She allowed her body to go floppy, so that I could do "whatever I wanted with her."

First, I blindfolded her. Seeing her lying there, unable to see me filled me with a feeling of strange power. Immediately, I felt aroused.

Second, I picked up the rope. I tied her wrists together, tightly so she couldn't move them at all. She moaned slightly as I did this. I slapped her lightly across the face.

We had a safe word. She'd told me she wanted me to be rough. I felt uneasy slapping her around the face but I knew it would give her pleasure.

I used the rope to tie her legs separately to each side of the bed. With them spread far apart, I had a great view of her cunt. Her clit was twitching and her vagina glistened with lubrication. I was tempted to fuck her there and then, but I knew that wasn't what she wanted. Not yet.

I picked up the nipple clamps that she'd requested. I looked at her perky tits. Her nipples were tiny; the clamps would almost entirely cover them. I leaned over and approached her with the first one.

I harnessed the strap-on around my crotch.

I clipped the clamp onto her hard nipple. She moaned again and I couldn't help but smile. I could tell how aroused she was by how erect her nipples were. I reached down and slapped her lightly on the clit.

I lifted the second clamp and put it on her other breast. She made a whimpering noise as I twisted it to make it tighter. Her nipple was squashed as the clamp pinched it.

Next, I took the flogger in my hand. I knew that she really wanted this, and the paddle. I stroked her naked body with the flogger. It was true that I was enjoying myself, too. I enjoyed looking at her naked body like this, knowing that I was giving her pleasure. I stroked her clamped breasts with the flogger and tingled with arousal myself. I tickled her clit with the flogger, then ran it down and back up her thighs.

Her body seemed like it was trying to move. I laughed and struck her for the first time.

She squealed and her body seemed like it was trying to escape again. I hit her again, across her clamped breast.

"Yes!" She moaned. That was the encouragement I needed. I struck her on the right breast, then the left, then right again.

She writhed beneath me and moaned. I looked at her clit. It was extremely erect.

I picked up the paddle. One side had studs and one was plain leather. I hit her pussy with the plain leather side. She screamed.

"Yes! Oh God!"

I hit her again, and again. She continued screaming and I turned over the paddle. I struck her pussy with the studded side. She moaned loudly, then her mouth stayed open.

I looked down at the strap-on. It was almost time to use it.

I rubbed my clit I struck her again with the studded side of the paddle. Her pussy was soaking wet and she was writhing with pleasure.

I walked around the side of the bed, approaching her with the strap-on pointing towards her mouth.

I pushed it into her mouth and she sucked it immediately. I thrust as she bobbed her head and took the rubber cock in mouth hungrily, not stopping for a breath once. I moaned as I watched the hunger in her face. I looked again at her glistening cunt. She sucked and sucked and I pushed the dildo in even further. Her hands were clenched in the rope and around her nipples looked red with soreness from the clamps. Her toes clenched and she sucked harder and harder.

I pulled the strap-on away from her, then slapped her around the face.

"Naughty, dirty, slut!" I said. I spat on her face.

She gasped and licked at her face. The spit was too far across her cheek for her tongue to reach.

"Dirty slut," I said again. "Whore."

I picked up the paddle.

I hit her breasts with the studded side. She screamed, then gritted her teeth. I hit her cunt. She gasped and shook her head. I hit it again. She moaned loudly. I stuck one finger into her soaking pussy, then hit her again with the paddle. Her body was shaking. I knew that it was time to make her come.

I put the paddle down and picked up our large vibrator. I turned it up to medium speed and ran it across her thighs. She moaned and pushed her pelvis up. She wanted me to touch her clit with it, I knew that. But I was going to make her wait.

I ran the vibrator up her body. It buzzed loudly as it touched the clamps. She moaned again. She was still writhing, desperate to feel it on her pussy.

Eventually, I moved the vibrator down to her clit. I pushed it into her.

"Oh God, yes! Yes!" She moaned loudly.

"Yes! Yes!"

I laughed and turned up the speed of the vibrator, to ¾ speed.

She gasped loudly.

"Yes! Yes!"

I moved the vibrator from side to side across her clit, then slapped her breasts again. She moaned and gasped more and started to squeal.

I turned the vibrator up to 100%. She screamed loudly as her legs started to buck violently. Her body lifted up and down and she kept screaming as she came powerfully on the vibrator. Her mouth stretched out sideways and her eyes screwed up as she shouted my name.

"Amanda! Oh God! Thank you, Amanda!"

"Mistress," I corrected her.

# In the Car

I was driving steadily when I felt her hand touch my leg. It wasn't the first time it had happened, but still, it took me by surprise. I turned to look at my co-worker's wife.

"Barbara," I said, "We're on the way to pick up your husband."

She smirked at me.

"I know," she said, daringly.

My clit twitched instantly and I knew I had no chance of talking her out of it. I kept driving.

Her hand went up my thigh and rested on my pussy.

"Mmm," she said, "I bet you're really wet under those clothes."

"Barbara," I said again, trying but failing to take control of the situation.

"Pull over," she said.

I looked at the time in the dashboard. We did have time to spare. We weren't picking Max up for another hour. If we kept going at this rate, we would be early.

She pushed her hand into my pussy.

Trying to stay calm, I looked in my mirrors. We were on a quiet street. The sun was coming down, but it was still technically light outside.

"Here?" I asked her.

"Right here," she said, "I need it. Now."

I looked in my mirrors again and hesitantly started to break. I shifted down my gears and stopped the car. She took off her seatbelt before I'd even pulled the handbrake, then climbed on top of me.

---

Barbara was frantic. She pulled her own underwear down and lifted her skirt. She grabbed my trousers and pulled them down. She pulled my panties and lowered herself onto me.

"I need you, now," she said again.

She straddled me started to fuck me. My shock quickly turned to pleasure. I pulled the top of her dress down and kissed her tits as she rode me. Our clits rubbed perfectly together again. She moaned loudly as she bounced up and down on top of me.

"Yes! Amanda!" She moaned, "I love fucking you! Your clit feels so good against mine!"

I grabbed her ass on top of me, then gripped her hair. She growled and moaned as she fucked me faster.

"Yes!" She said, "Harder! Harder!"

She rode me enthusiastically, pushing her body into mine. I felt the lubrication from her warm, wet pussy. Her smooth legs rubbed across my thighs. I stroked her legs and spanked her ass.

"YES!" She screamed as I spanked her again "YESSS!"

I spanked her even more as she kept riding me. Together, we got faster and faster. Despite being in the middle of the street, our inhibitions were nonexistent. We fucked faster and faster and I knew I was going to come. I wanted her to come, first.

I reached around and slapped her ass. She was still moaning loudly and I slapped her again. I poked my finger into her ass. I was about to come.

I stuck my finger in Barbara's ass as she rode me and she started to scream. I felt her vagina spasming and I knew she was coming. I fucked her ass with my finger as I screamed and came with her. She slowed down on top of me and pulled my face into hers. She kissed me passionately and I felt her breathing start to slow down. I pulled my finger slowly out of her ass and she climbed off of me. Still slightly breathless, she climbed off of me and back into the passenger seat.

"That was incredible," she said.

I wordlessly agreed, nodding my head as I looked for my panties.

## Alley Way

I knew when we left the bar that we wouldn't make it to hers. We were just too horny.

It was just two streets from her house, though, that we couldn't take it any more.

"Come in here," she said, "I know a place."

I followed her, blindly, into a dark alleyway. We kissed heavily for the millionth time that night and I ran my hand up her skirt.

"Are you sure?" I asked her, not that I needed to.

She nodded and pulled me into her. She lifted her left leg up around me. I lifted both of her thighs so that her legs were wrapped around me and pushed her into the wall of the alleyway. My fingers dug into her crotch.

"Push them in me," she whispered into my ear.

Holding her up with one hand, I pushed two fingers towards her hungry pussy. She wore a thong, but I moved it to one side. I stuck my fingers inside and moaned as I felt how warm and wet she was.

"Oh God. Yes! Yes!" She moaned as I started to fuck her with my hand. We kissed again. I moaned into her mouth. It felt so good, feeling inside her pussy. I'd been aching for her all evening. Finally we could feel this sensual pleasure.

"Yeaah," she moaned into my shoulder. Pushed against the wall, she couldn't move. Her hand rested around my pussy. She stroked my clit.

"Oh, baby!" She said as I fucked her hard with my fingers. It crossed my mind that somebody might walk past but I didn't care that much. This felt so good. I pushed my fingers in and out of her again, starting a steady rhythm.

She moaned steadily and kissed my neck. Her fingers were now inside my panties, rubbing my horny clit. Both of our breathing was heavy as we fingered each other. Her legs were cold but smooth and the warmth of her pussy was amazing contrasted with the outdoor temperature. I focused on the pleasure: hers and mine. We reached orgasm quickly out there in the alleyway that night before heading to hers. I on her hand and she orgasmed strongly with my fingers inside her. As I pulled them out of her, she whispered to me,

"Thanks for the starter..."

## Main Course

At her apartment, she told me that we would have the 'main course'. I was already at the maximum level of horny again as we walked through the door.

I'd been there before, several times, but it still felt exciting each time we entered together. This woman lived in a small apartment, above a shop outside of town. She had a small living room and a larger bedroom. We went straight to the bedroom, as we always did.

She pushed me onto the bed and sensually pulled off my blouse. Now we'd got our urgent 'starter' out of our systems, we could afford to take our time. My lover laid my blouse beside me, unhooked my bra. She kissed my breasts, one by one.

"I love your nipples," she said, licking my right nipple playfully.

I laughed. "Not as much as I love yours," I said. I unzipped her dress at the back and she helped me to pull it over her head. We kissed again before I unhooked her bra at the back. I pulled the straps down her shoulders, then kissed each of her breasts softly.

"I really do love your nipples," I said, nibbling softly on each of them.

She laughed and lay back on the bed. Her thong was in place again now, but was soaking wet from her natural lubrication.

I pulled her thong down and kissed her pussy. She moaned gently. I kissed her there again, and again.

I kissed all the way down her leg, to her foot. I kissed her feet, one by one, then all the way up her other leg.

She sat up and leaned towards me. She unbuttoned my jeans and pulled them down slowly. She smiled when she saw my soaked panties.

"I'm glad you're ready for action," she said.

She pulled my panties down, making me fully naked. She pulled me onto the bed with her.

We kissed again, slowly and lovingly. Her tongue explored my mouth as mine did hers. I ran my hand down her warm back, then rested it on her ass. She stroked my tits and torso, then ran her hands up my thighs, stroking my my vulva and teasing my clitoris. She reached around and grabbed my ass, then explored my back with her fingertips. Already, I was in sensual heaven.

My pussy throbbed close to hers. She pushed herself into me. I knew she was feeling ready again. I reached down and put my finger into her.

She moaned gently and kissed me strongly. I ran my other hand through her dark hair as I pleasured her again with my hand. She was soaking wet and her pussy was hot. I moaned with her as I pushed my finger in and out of her.

I reached for her clit and began to stroke it gently. We were in no rush, not any more. I stroked it softly and kept it slow. She moaned and pushed her head into my shoulder.

"Yes," she moaned, "Like that."

Her eyes were closed as she lay on me whilst I stroked her clit. I rubbed it from side to side, then up and down. Occasionally, I poked at the entry to her vagina. Each time I did, her body jerked expectantly. I rubbed her clit again.

"Yes, like that."

This time, I didn't stop. As I rubbed and rubbed, I watched her beside me. She smiled and her body relaxed into mine. She lay on me, filled with trust as her pleasure grew. Her breathing started to get shorter and she gripped onto me suddenly.

"Don't stop!" She said.

I rubbed her faster, then, keeping my hand in the same position.

"Oh! God!" She moaned. I kept rubbing her, watching her as she reached her climax. She moaned my name loudly and pulled me into her. Her body spasmed next to mine and she kissed my forehead.

"You're amazing," she said to me, kissing me again, "You're amazing."

I kissed her and climbed on top of her.

---

She was even wetter than before. I reached to the table by her bed and picked up one of our vibrators. Her legs wrapped around my body and she held her hands above her head. I turned it on and put it between our clits.

"Yes," I moaned, "Oh God, I love sharing this with you!"

"I love feeling your pussy close to mine," she moaned, "Oh yeah! I love your pussy!"

I thrust on top of her in a steady rhythm, pushing the vibrator against both of our clits. She moved her hips with me and we both moaned together.

"This is so good," she said.

I looked down at her pretty, fair face and light hair. She was gorgeous. I loved making love to this woman. Her eyes shone and she always looked at me with real passion. I kissed her again.

We continued to thrust together and her breasts pushed into mine. Our nipples were both fully erect. I moaned as her nipple touched mine and she reached down and grabbed my ass. She spanked me lightly, then reached for my anus. I gasped.

She poked her finger into my anus as we fucked and I gasped some more.

"Oh! God!" I moaned as she pushed it in even further.

"You like that, baby?" She said.

"Yes! Yes!" I moaned, still gasping.

I thrust against the vibrator and her faster and faster and felt myself becoming faint with pleasure.

"Oh!" I moaned again. She was thrusting into me hard now and fucking my ass quickly with her finger. The pleasure I felt overwhelmed me and tingling sensations spread throughout my entire ass and crotch.

"Oh God!" I moaned again. I felt my own face beginning to distort.

"Yeah, baby!" She moaned, "Come! Come inside me! Come for me!"

I inhaled sharply, then exhaled as I started to orgasm.

"Oh!" I moaned again as I came on top of my lover.

"Yes," she said encouragingly, still poking my anus with her finger.

"Yes, come for me baby," she said.

She slid her finger out of my ass and stroked my back, hugging me tightly.

"I love it when you come for me," she said.

# Annabelle

Some people say that one night stands are never really that good. Personally, I don't think that's true. Especially when you meet girls like Annabelle.

---

Annabelle was a busty girl with a lot of confidence. She had long, blonde hair and long, tanned legs. She wore revealing clothes regularly and she really, truly didn't care what people thought of her. When we ended up dancing together, in a club, I had a feeling that the night was going to be a good one!

---

"You look pretty cute, in your lesbian clothes!" She'd said to me. I'd laughed loudly.

"Well, I am a lesbian," I'd told her.

"Good," she'd said.

I had looked down, a tiny bit self-consciously, at my outfit. I wore a black t-shirt with dark camo trousers and trainers. Was I being too much of a lesbian stereotype?

She saw me looking at myself and slapped my arm.

"I was just messing," she said.

We continued to dance.

---

Annabelle's body ground up mine and our hips moved together as we danced. I knew she knew I wanted her, and she knew I knew she knew. That's

209

what made our dancing get even hotter. She shook her breasts flirtatiously at me and lifted her thigh so that it stroked the side of mine. She wore a short, black dress with no tights or stockings beneath it. She wore black, strappy sandals that were extremely high. She was torturing me with her hotness. I needed to fuck her.

After several more songs, I asked her how long she was planning on staying out for. She looked me boldly in the eye and said,

"Until I get offered a good fuck."

I didn't say a word as I stared back into her eyes. We held each other's gaze for almost a minute, before I said.

"Are you coming, then?"

We held hands as we walked out of the door.

---

I took Annabelle in a taxi back to my place. The second we walked through the door, she pushed me up against the wall. She kissed me firmly and dominantly.

"I knew I'd get you," she said, "I wanted you since the second I set eyes on you."

She kissed me again, pulling my black t-shirt over her head, then stepped away from me as I stood in my bra. She took off her shoes and walked into my apartment.

"Nice apartment," she said, "I like it here."

"Thanks," I said, standing staring at her "Would you like a drink?"

She looked at me, then stared at my tits. She licked her lips.

"Got any orange juice?" She asked casually.

"Sure," I said, starting to walk to the kitchen.

"Great, then I'd like some in the morning, please," she said, smiling at me cheekily. "Water will do for now."

I grabbed us both a bottle of water from the fridge and threw them into my bedroom.

"Come on," I said, grabbing her and kissing her passionately.

I pushed Annabelle onto my bed, then carried on kissing her. Her leg wrapped around my body and she moaned as she pushed herself into me. She unhooked my bra and squeezed my tits.

"Got any toys?" She asked

I nodded. She reached down to unbutton my trousers. I moaned as she stroked my hard clit.

"Get them," she said, "I want you to penetrate me."

I pulled out a new dildo from my drawer. It was huge. Almost 10 inches in length. She looked at it excitedly.

"Yes," she said, "Fuck me with that!"

She grabbed the dildo, still stroking my clit.

I gasped as she pleasured me and I pushed the dildo into her hungry pussy. She screamed loudly.

"Yes! Yes! Fuck me!"

I pushed the dildo in and out of her. Watching her glistening vagina eat it up. She moaned deeply and continuously.

I moaned again as she rubbed me harder. We looked into each other's eyes.

"Fuck me harder," she moaned.

I pushed the dildo into her even harder and faster. She still wore her black dress, but it was pulled up around her body. I wanted to see her tits. Leaving the dildo inside her, I pulled her dress over her head. She growled and helped me to pull it off her.

"Fuck me!" She demanded again, "I need it! I need you to fuck me!"

I pushed the dildo even further into her and penetrated her hard. She pushed two fingers into my soaked pussy. She still wore her bra.

I moaned as I told her, "I need to see your tits!"

She reached around with one hand and unhooked her bra, tearing it off. I moaned as she continued to finger me and I saw her bare breasts beneath me. Her tits were massive and her nipples were also quite large and very hard. I leant forward to suck them.

I pulled her body into my face as I sucked her tits. I licked each nipple and all around her large bosom. She continued to gasp as I fucked her hard with the dildo.

Suddenly, I pulled away from her. I wanted to see her on top. As though she read my mind, she pushed me onto my back.

"My turn to ride!" she said.

The dildo was between us. She grabbed it in her hand and pushed it towards my pussy. I moaned with anticipation, before she even entered.

I kissed her breasts again and grabbed onto her bare ass. I spanked her and she squealed.

"Naughty!" She said to me, pinching my nipples. I also squealed. She slapped my tits.

Annabelle grabbed onto the dildo and held it right in front of her pussy. She started to rub her clit with one end and mine with the other.

"Oh yeah," she said, "You want me to fuck you, don't you?"

She pushed the dildo to the edge of my vagina. I needed it inside me.

"Annabelle," I gasped.

She moved it across my clit again, then pushed it slowly into my pussy.

"Time for me to fuck you," she said, staring into my eyes again.

---

As she entered me with the dildo, we both groaned loudly. She started to grind on top of me and I moved my hips to thrust with her. I ran my fingers down her back and gripped her ass. I spanked her playfully and she moaned even louder. I spanked her harder.

She bounced on top of me with amazing energy. She just seemed to get faster and faster and faster. She was like a machine, but with the softness of what she was: a beautiful woman. She bounced up and down on me, pushing the dildo in deeply. I moaned loudly each time she thrust, as she hit my G-spot. She stroked my tits and looked down at me as she fucked me. I kissed her massive tits. She smothered me with them, still grinding into me. I moaned into her cleavage and spanked her again. She sat up and rode me even faster. Her clit kept hitting mine as she fucked me deeply with the dildo.

"I'm going to come!" She yelled.

She bounced up and down on me, gripping my chest.

"I'm coming!" She said.

Her breasts bounced up and down and her mouth opened wide. She screamed as her body started to spasm on top of mine.

"Oh! God!" She yelled.

As she came violently on me, her vagina started to pulsate. The sight of her coming, combined with the intense pleasure I felt, made me come immediately. I pulled her body into mine as I screamed and came with her. My body also spasmed without control.

She kissed my lips softly, before climbing off me. She pulled the dildo out of me and slapped my thigh with it. As she walked away to use the bathroom, I admired her full buttocks. She was an exceptional woman.

# Anal

I love asses. It doesn't matter what shape and size they are (within reason), they're invariably hot.

It's for that reason, that anal sex will always be an indulgence I find it impossible to decline.

---

I was working one day, when a woman in her early 30s tried to steal some lipstick. This was a common occurrence, and I was used to dealing with petty theft attempts. I put my hand on the woman's shoulder and watched her blush with shame.

"Come on," I said to her. I led her to my office.

---

In the office, she was full of remorse, as they often are. I half-listened, half-looked at the woman. She had dark hair, currently wore lipstick (of the same shade she was trying to nick!) and she was dressed casually, in jeans and a black t-shirt.

"I'm so sorry," she said, "I don't know what came over me. I've never done anything like that before. Please, please, can you not tell anybody? Please? I'll pay! I'm a teacher. I can't have a record."

I imagined the woman teaching a class. Right now, she seemed desperate and far from in control. I tried to imagine her being in charge.

"A teacher?" I asked.

"Yes," she said, with tears in her eyes, "I'm a middle school teacher."

She started to sob.

I put my hand on her shoulder.

"It's okay," I said, "Shh, it's okay."

I sat down next to her.

"We might be able to come to some kind of arrangement."

---

She bent over my desk with her jeans around her ankles. I stroked her ass with one hand, as I reached for my strap-on.

"Very nice ass," I said, "Beautiful."

The woman had stopped crying, and by this point she was aroused.

"I've never been fucked by a woman," she said into the desk. I laughed and poked her ass with the strap-on.

"You're about to be," I said.

I reached around and felt her pussy. She was wet and seemed tight. I wanted to fuck her there, but she needed to be fucked up the ass.

I pushed my finger into her pussy. She moaned loudly. I pushed another one in an penetrated her with two fingers. She moaned more and pushed her ass back into the strap-on.

*She really does want it*, I remember thinking.

I pulled my fingers out of her soaking pussy and rubbed them on her asshole.

"Yess!" She moaned. I pushed them in slowly. She moaned deeply and her arms fell forward on the table. I pulled them out, then pushed them in again. Her ass was tight and warm.

I took my fingers out of her ass, then spat on it. I spat on my hand and wet the strap-on. Then I pushed it inside her.

She screamed as the rubber cock entered her. I started to thrust slowly and she moaned loudly. I put my hand around her mouth.

"Shh," I told her. She slobbered over my hand and kept moaning into it.

As I thrust in and out of her ass, she started to relax. Her ass seemed to get hungrier and hungrier for the strap-on. After several more thrusts, her body was moving with mine.

"Oh yeah," I said as I saw her ass bouncing on my crotch. "Oh God, yeah baby. Yeah your ass likes to get fucked!"

"Fuck my ass!" She moaned, "Oh God, yes! Fuck my ass! Yes!"

I thrust more quickly in and out of her and reached around to stroke her clit. She screamed again. I took my hand off her clit and spanked her.

I grabbed onto both of her buttocks as I pounded into her.

"Fuck yes!" I said, "Fuck yes!"

I fucked her faster and spanked each of her buttocks. I reached for my phone, that was near her on the desk. I took a photo of me fucking her ass.

I rubbed her clit again and she squealed. Her body started to shake as I rubbed it faster and kept pounding her ass.

"Yes," she moaned, "Yes! Yes!"

I kept fucking her and rubbing her clit. Her body shook violently and I knew she was going to come. I shouldn't let her, not yet. I pulled the strap-on out of her and let go of her clit.

Urgently, she reached down to her own clit. She started to rub herself frantically as I looked down at her. I took a couple more photos, but she couldn't stop.

"Oh! God! No!" She moaned.

I laughed and put the camera down. I reached down and rubbed her clit for her.

She moaned and bucked in front of me. Orgasming strongly on the desk, she reached behind and grabbed my ass.

"Oh yes," she moaned, still absorbed in sensual pleasure, "Oh yeah."

I stepped back from her and looked at her ass again. She had red marks where I'd spanked her and her asshole looked raw.

She stood up slowly, then looked at me with concern.

"Am I let off?" She asked nervously, remembering why she'd ended up there.

I nodded at her slowly.

"You're let off," I told her.

She pulled up her jeans and looked at me timidly.

"Thank you," she said.

"My pleasure," I replied, smiling.

To be continued...